## PRAISE FOR SB E

"If you wonder about the eth(
future, let Auden be your wind
tale; one part AI and Robot take
*in the Rye.* Auden is as authentic as the everyday person confronted by changing times. Near-future Toronto exists in a timeline I can see happening, one where the major question of life isn't 'what sort of job will I have', but 'what will I do once it's gone?'
A triumphant debut by thought-provoking and imaginative SB Edwards."
Sapha Burnell, *Author of NEON Lieben, & the Judge of Mystics Saga*

"The fact that it's not about the machines trying to kill us all is a breath of fresh air in a media landscape dominated by fears of technology rather than people using it. In other words, you shouldn't be afraid of the hammer...
Overall, it's a very interesting book that gave me a lot to think about, and I think you should read it, too."
*EvilRoda, Goodreads*

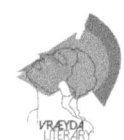

**Vraeyda Literary**
An Imprint of
Vraeyda Media Inc
Port Coquitlam, BC
www.vraeydamedia.ca

Copyright © 2024 by SB Edwards

All rights reserved.

No part of this publication may be reproduced, distributed, or transmitted in any form or by any means, including photocopying, recording, or other electronic or mechanical methods, without the prior written permission of the publisher, except as permitted by Canada or U.S. copyright law. For permission requests, contact Vraeyda Literary.

The story, all names, characters, and incidents portrayed in this production are fictitious. No identification with actual persons (living or deceased), places, buildings, and products is intended or should be inferred.

Book Cover by Emily Armstrong
Illustrations by Sapha Burnell

ISBN (Paperback): 978-1-988034-64-5
ISBN (eBook): 978-1-988034-50-8
ISBN (Hardcover): 978-1-988034-51-5

First edition 2024

Printed in Canada

Vraeyda Literary books are published by Vraeyda Media Inc, A113-2099 Lougheed HWY, Port Coquitlam, BC.

10 9 8 7 6 5 4 3 2 1

SB EDWARDS

# THE BOTTOM LINE

Ad postero
Lucentus es spero

They hit me straight in the back like bullets squeezed off from an assassin lying in wait. Three shots disrupting my already frantic morning as I stepped out of the maglev and onto the filthy old platform at Dufferin station.

"Hey! Hey buddy!"

The smell hit me soon after, carried along by the wind of the maglev leaving the station. A sour, wicked stench, like a colony of termites inside a felled tree, half-digested, invaded my nostrils and stabbed at it with dozens of tiny, putrid daggers. Though it had been years, I recognized the smell immediately, and resisted the urge to throw up in my mouth.

His name was Ignatius. A short, greasy old acquaintance who approached me as though he was in as much of a hurry as I was. I hadn't seen him in years. If I'd made a list of the people I wanted to deal with that morning, he'd be on the absolute bottom.

Like a kid in a public school cafeteria singled out by the principal for having started the food fight, I looked around hoping he was accusing the guy beside me. But the only other person on the platform was an old lady doddering toward the elevator.

Hardly someone you'd call "buddy."

The fact that I was innocent was irrelevant—it could be nobody but me. I had no choice but to accept this unjust punishment.

His polo shirt, which may or may not have once been white, looked as though it had been plucked from his big brother's laundry pile to wear to his first job interview as a teenager. And his first day at work, and every other day of his life for the following twenty years. A mosaic of patterns from every medium imaginable. A deeply embedded chronicle of all the stain-capable substances that entered his orbit. Some I recognized, some I didn't, one I hoped was ketchup.

His was the type of personal style that could only have been cultivated by someone who spent his entire life in a career where you couldn't possibly be the worst dressed no matter how hard you tried.

"Auden, hey buddy! On your way to work, huh?" he said through a half-chewed tuna sandwich. He launched a chunk of onion from his mouth, which stuck to my jacket like a popped whitehead to a bathroom mirror.

"Oh, sorry about that buddy." He pawed at it with a mustard-stained hand, trying to clean it up, but only making things worse.

I pushed his hand away, adding a blotch of yellow to the book I was holding—a well-worn copy of *The Iliad*—in the process. At least I was almost done reading it; the smell of mustard would only accompany me during Hector's funeral. "It's fine, Iggy. And yeah, I'm going to work. In fact, I'm running behind, and—"

"You still doing the crane on that construction crew? Working on that high rise on Eglinton? Must be nice buddy. I was doing maintenance at the hospital until I got bottom lined last month. Now I spend all day at home with the old lady and it's driving me nuts buddy. I'm so bored I can't stand it! It's like one of those old shows from a hundred years ago where the husband and wife hate each other but they're stuck because no one else will have them, you know buddy? What's that old fashioned show called, where the husband says he's going to beat up his wife on the Moon or something? You know which show I'm talking about buddy? My grandma used to watch it when I was a kid because she said her grandma used to watch it but I always thought it was a weird show, you know buddy? Anyway it's hard to find something to do with all this spare time buddy, I'm used to working all day and now I have all this spare time with nothing to do. What would you do with this much time? It can't be long before you get bottom lined too, huh?"

Listening to him was like reading an essay from a student who'd outlined a perfectly coherent idea in six pages for a teacher who demanded ten. Or a person who's competing to see how many words they could cram into a single breath.

"I don't know, Iggy" I interrupted mid-ramble. "Maybe you should get a hobby."

My face and breath began to reveal my frustration, a signal as foreign to the receiver as petroleum to an aloo-cab—neither recognized nor desired. "Anyway, I really—"

"I did buddy! I still get up early in the morning and do stuff around town and I set up a big saltwater fish tank at home and now I carve stuff out of scrap wood and sell it on the internet but there's only so much I can do before the old lady starts nagging me again. 'Ignatius, did you take out the garbage? Ignatius, did you clean the autovac? Ignatius, did you refill the food printer yet?' Nag nag nag man, it's driving me crazy! It's like-"

"I need to go Iggy. See you later."

I tapped him on the shoulder with my book as I walked away, in the hopes of returning at least some of his mustard.

"Call me buddy, let's get a beer or something!" he shouted after me. I pretended not to hear him.

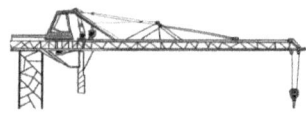

The universe had, it seemed, aligned itself perfectly to ensure my lateness that morning. Ignatius was just the latest in a parade of frustrations.

I boarded the escalator only to run into the next obstacle: a gaggle of people standing across it as it crawled upward, an extra hour's worth of seconds to wait and think about how late I was, how I'd explain it to Byron, my boss, how these people should stay on one side of the escalator and let people who are in a hurry pass.

What time was it anyway? I pulled out my phone to check the time, but the screen was blurred. A bright blue beam emitted from the phone, drawing a tube of light around me. Sounds began to blend in with smells, sights became tastes. Nothing and everything existed at once.

An image came into focus.

The sky, like a melted blue slushie, unnaturally vibrant and sickeningly sweet. The ground, an impeccably manicured lawn, bright and uniform as a puddle of antifreeze. A young couple, attractive but not too attractive, atop a blanket adorned in a red and white checker pattern underneath the only tree in sight: a lush, green maple. Beside them, a brown wicker picnic basket. The woman reached in and pulled out a box of Snappy Cake© gourmet cakes.

She broke off a piece, placing it in the man's mouth and smearing a bit of icing across his lips as she pulled away. She threw her head back in an exaggerated laugh. So did the man. In the background, a bird chirped. They both turned to the camera, aiming their plastic smiles and empty eyes right at me. "New cherry flavoured Snappy Cake© gourmet cakes," said a charmingly average voice over the couple's rigor mortis grins, "available at your local grocer."

*These new subway ads are so weird.* I bought one box of those damn Snappy Cake things a couple of years ago, and they still wouldn't stop hounding me to buy more. Maybe I would, too, if they didn't keep constantly bugging me, or if they didn't taste like a ball of rubber bands.

The Ad-Ex advertising system scanned my eyes and dug into all the information it collected about me over the years to find another fantasy, another insecurity upon which it could prey.

Then it tapped into my phone's projector, creating a display that surrounded me. No matter where I looked, all I could see was my own body and the Ad-Ex display. After the Snappy Cake ad had faded, a new world flashed across the screen.

A green-skinned warrior stood defiantly atop a boulder. Blood dripped from his spear, his shield, his enormous teeth jutting out of his under-bitten jaw. His bronze plumed helmet glistened in the sun, out of which his black hair, dreadlocked by filth and blood, dangled like rotten grapes on a dead vine. He unleashed an inhuman roar and hurled his spear forward, slicing through the red sky, as luminous as a trillion-watt exit sign. A blur of creatures followed the spear.

An assorted mass of all shapes, sizes, and number of limbs charged to battle, colliding with the interlocked shields of a group of humans standing in glistening plated armour as the image faded to smoke and blackness.

A door opened. A beam of light cut through the darkness, tempered by the silhouette of the first modern human to enter this eons-neglected space. After her first breath filled her lungs with stale, rancid air, she covered her mouth with a scarf to filter the rest. One hand on her flashlight, another on her knife cradled in a sheath outside her right thigh, she crept forward.

Flecks of dust drifted across the flashlight's beam, in motion as reluctantly as a lazy house cat pushed off a chair. It reflected back at her. A signal she'd found what she was after, a golden artifact no larger than a wine bottle, or one of those showbiz awards they once gave out. She put a hand on either side of the glass encasing it, and the room began to shake. Dust and pebbles fell from the ceiling as the image faded to smoke and blackness.

A young man stood in the crow's nest of a ship, a life of relentless sunshine and battle adding decades to his otherwise youthful face. A tattered but defiant Jolly Roger waved in the wind above him. He peered through a telescope into the distance.

"Enemy off the starboard bow!" On the deck, his fellow crew members dragged cannonballs over to a series of black cannon arranged along the ship's starboard. The navigator spun the wheel, bringing the enemy ship into view of the guns. Cannon flashes paired with explosions on the enemy's ship, sending debris and sailors flying into the air. The image faded to smoke and darkness.

"You can experience all these adventures yourself, and more" a disembodied announcer's voice told me as an image of the LifeSim system appeared. "For just three easy payments of $499.99, you can do this too, right now. Just nod your head and we'll debit your account and send you your LifeSim NuREALity package. Go ahead, simply nod your head and take your first step toward living the lives you've always dreamed about, today."

My head remained perfectly still, but my clenched fist trembled. Why couldn't I have remembered to take the other escalator, the one with the normal old-fashioned poster ads stuck along the walls? The one old people took so they wouldn't have a heart attack from the unexpected terror of suddenly finding oneself in the middle of a battle with a collection of fiendish hell beasts?

Finally off the escalator, the Ad-Ex turned off, and I broke into a jog. Outside, the warm April breeze mixed with the smell of sizzling meat—or, some sort of protein in tube form. It reminded me of my empty stomach. An aloo sold hot dogs from a stand, in the artificial sunbeam reflected off one of the dozens of massive condo buildings that popped up in the area in recent decades. I wished I'd had time to stop for one.

I pulled out my phone, and wished I'd replaced the piece of duct tape over the holoprojector lens after watching some HoloTube last night. I know it sounds strange, but a piece of tape could block the projector lens entirely. They could project through the pocket of my jeans or my jacket, so why can't they project through duct tape? No idea, but it works.

Draven, one of the guys on the crew at work, told us about it a few months back. He doesn't even have a phone—says it's a surveillance device so the government can monitor our movements. He might be right, who knows. But if the government, or anyone else for that matter, wanted to find me, they wouldn't have too difficult a time.

I opened Rush-Kii, and requested an aloo-cab to take me to work. Under normal circumstances I'd have walked from the subway—it was the only real exercise I ever got—but I was already 10 minutes late. I didn't want to add any more. The app alerted me that aloo-cab number 6289 was, conveniently, sitting right in front of the station.

I got in and took a seat on one of the pair of three-person benches facing each other. Always thought they resembled one of those old-fashioned horse-drawn carriages in movies, but only the benches. No horse pulled it, and no human drove it, since cabs hadn't been operated by actual people in decades and cars hadn't been dragged by horses in a lot longer, probably like 150 years. Unless you're on one of those cliché romantic getaways with your spouse on vacation in Central Park or something.

I don't remember ever taking a cab with a human driver, though I'd never been an avid user of the taxi cab system in general, and neither had my parents when I was a kid so I guess I never had much exposure.

"WELCOME TO YOUR RUSH-KII AY ELL YEW CAB," the cab announced in an absurdly bright and pleasant voice, as though it was mere moments away from screaming or weeping, so great is the joy filling its soul. "THIS CAB WAS HIRED BY MX. AUDEN BLACK. PLEASE CONFIRM YOUR IDENTITY MATCHES THIS DESCRIPTION BY USING YOUR VOICEPRINT."

"Yes, hi, it's me, Auden Black."

"THANK YOU FOR YOUR CONFIRMATION, MX. BLACK. PLEASE CONFIRM YOUR DESTINATION. YOU HAVE REQUESTED TRANSPORTATION TO THE ADDRESS ONE SIX NINE THREE DUFFERIN STREET, TORONTO, ONTARIO, CANADA, POSTAL CODE M6X 3L7. IS THIS CORRECT?"

"Yes, for god's sake, let's go already."

"THANK YOU FOR YOUR CONFIRMATION, MX. BLACK. OUR ESTIMATED TIME OF ARRIVAL IS SEVEN SEVENTEEN AM. PLEASE NOTE THAT I CANNOT BEGIN YOUR JOURNEY UNTIL YOUR SEATBELT IS SECURELY FASTENED."

I whipped the seatbelt across my body, and fumbled with the buckle a few times like a drunk trying to open the lock with the wrong key after an eventful night. I took a deep breath to calm myself, and heard the belt click.

The cab smelled like a mixture of coffee, cheap cologne, and olives. A stew of the latter floated in brine mixed with chunks of glass on the floor. Must have been from the last rider who made a mess and didn't want to be stuck with the cleaning bill. I considered reporting it, but it might have been two or three or four or even ten riders ago.

No one wanted to report it out of fear they'd get blamed and have to foot the bill. I'd never reported anything before, so I didn't know if I'd get blamed. Then again, the next person might, and it might still fall on me.

There should be an option to report a mess that someone else made, but if there were, everyone would probably report someone else. Or maybe there should be security cameras in the cabs so you can prove you didn't do it. People wouldn't want to take an aloo-cab if they thought someone was watching them the whole time, or maybe there actually were security cameras and they were hidden.

I decided not to report the olives. Or rather, I couldn't decide what to do and my inaction spoke for itself.

"THANK YOU FOR FASTENING YOUR SEATBELT, MX. BLACK. WE WILL NOW DEPART. ARE YOU COMFORTABLE?"

"Yes damn it, just go!"

On the window beside me, a translucent screen displayed a number of news headlines which floated past, with an option to open the article to find out more. They blurred with the scenery as the aloo-cab manoeuvred through the traffic.

*Two injured in accident at Pape and Danforth between a cyclist and Regal Condominium Corporation.*

*Archaeologists discover cache of previously unknown writings from Roman emperor Titus in Eris Industries Aloo Repair Depot.*

*Mars mission Juno lands safely in Capital Espresso Bar with several tonnes of gold.*

*HIV vaccine entering third clinical trial, Rite Hardware Dispensary optimistic about results.*

*Aloo firefighting teams have controlled the spread of wildfires in Izakaya Sushi House.*

*Canadians collecting bottom line now reaches 22 million.*

"RIDE REQUEST DETECTED. WE WILL BE TAKING A SLIGHT DETOUR DOWN HALLAM STREET TO DOVERCOURT ROAD, THEN SOUTH TO BLOOR WHERE WE WILL PICK UP OUR NEXT PASSENGER IN THE POOL. THEY HAVE REQUESTED A RIDE TO THE AREA NEAR OAKWOOD AVENUE AND SAINT CLAIR AVENUE WEST. BASED ON THIS ALTERATION IN PLANS, YOUR MODIFIED ESTIMATED TIME OF ARRIVAL IS SEVEN THIRTY-SEVEN AM. THANK YOU FOR YOUR PATIENCE AND UNDERSTANDING."

## 2

"What are you doing here so early?" Byron walked around the corner of a pile of steel beams to thwart my attempt to sneak onto the job site. The foreman of our crew, Byron was built like a football player, or a security guard at a fancy nightclub, or a mafia muscle man, or a giant lump of concrete. His face, framed at the bottom by a long greying beard hanging down past his shirt collar and at the top by a neon green hardhat seated atop his receding hairline, wore a perpetual scowl which belied his mostly amicable nature.

If he were my girlfriend's dad, I'd be terrified of him. But thankfully he's not—he's my boss, and in that role, he's easy to live with.

"What do you mean? I'm ten minutes late." I was a lot later than that, really, but decided to exaggerate in my favour.

"Yeah but we got a meeting," he said in his New Jersey accent. "By the way you uh, you got some mustard on your jacket there."

I'd forgotten. Our normal shifts started at seven, but when we had staff meetings Byron scheduled them for eight. No one bothered to do much work during that hour; most of the crew sat around chatting, and Byron didn't mind. He also didn't mind when I stayed home and slept in. I could have avoided a whole parade of annoyances this morning.

Oh well.

The food trailer, at least, could solve one of my problems. It was an old camping trailer—or what was left of it—that sat on a pile of cinder blocks next door to

Byron's much nicer office trailer. Like that of an abandoned farmhouse, the door pattered against the trailer in the breeze. You'd think one of the carpenters nearby would have fixed it. But instead, it dangled from the half roll worth of weathered duct tape that kept it attached. The walls and ceiling were slowly rotting away, replaced by whatever spare materials they slapped on.

I often wondered how much of the original was left.

The equipment inside wasn't much better, reflecting the diminutive budget the company gave for such things. Most of it didn't matter; the only difference between a fridge or reverse microwave from 20 years ago and the modern ones was the extra doodads we didn't need. Like the ones that chopped up your food, or had a built-in system to order some tomatoes when you started to run low, or monitored your diet and recommended improvements to your nutritional intake. That, and energy efficiency, but none of us were paying the power bills.

The only real difference was the crummy old food printer. I wouldn't be surprised if it was the first one, but I'm no historian.

Remember when they first started opening restaurants that served replicated food? And how awful it tasted? I'm pretty sure they bought this food printer for cheap from one of the places that closed down. A neon pink fluorescent sign, "Replik-Eat" was written across the top. Still worked too, if you plugged it in. It offered three items on its menu: a "bacon" and "egg" sandwich, "pancakes," or a bowl of "oatmeal." Along with your meal, you had a choice between "orange juice," "tea," or "coffee," the button for the last of which was buried in a patina of grime so thick it obscured the label.

I pressed the coffee and sandwich buttons and watched as the sandwich emerged from a puddle of uniform beige goo inside the machine. Like a time-lapse video of a frozen block of pancake batter melting in reverse. Absolutely revolting. The fact you could see the process is one of the reasons why these early food printers never took off.

Well that, and the flavour. We had syrup, brown sugar, and cinnamon to add to the oatmeal and the pancakes, but it wasn't possible to improve on the flavour.

To get an idea of what the oatmeal was like, here's a fun experiment you can try at home. Head down to your local carpentry shop and sweep the floor until you have enough sawdust to fill a cereal bowl. Boil some water and pour it into the sawdust. Stir until it's fully mixed. Now look at what you have in the kitchen and see what you can add to it to make it taste good.

Substitute the sawdust in the above experiment for an old, crumbly sponge and you've got a good idea of what the pancakes were like.

The only thing that approached palatability was the sandwich. Slathered in ketchup, you could bury the "egg" and "cheese" flavours and turn it into the sort of thing you could eat if you had slept through your alarm and didn't have time to grab breakfast. Somehow, though, the "bacon" was a decent copy of the real thing.

I don't think the machine actually printed the coffee as much as it dispensed it the same way instant coffee works. Same with the orange juice and tea. Their quality rivalled that of the rest of the machine's creations, but even bad coffee is better than none.

"You try that shit yet?" one of the new apprentices asked me as I grabbed my pale, soulless sandwich, as though a vampire had sucked the life out of it. Normally, the food printer had packs of food colouring to at least make the sandwiches look like a real piece of food, but no one bothered replacing it. What a ridiculous question—I'd just pulled it out of the printer and there weren't any bites. And I'd been working on this crew for fifteen years, of course I've had it before.

What was this kid's name? Oh well, he'd be gone in a few weeks anyway. Most of them were.

"They got some new flavour goo for that thing. It tastes a bit less like fuckin' dog shit now."

Like a fresh arrival at a maximum-security prison, the new guys often tried to make sure everyone knew how tough they were. This particular new guy cussed a lot, and wore a denim vest with cut off sleeves over a button up flannel shirt in red and black plaid. He made a point of trying to grow a beard too, but all he could manage was a sparse forest around his mouth with a few lonely sprigs on his cheeks.

"Oh and hey, you've got some shit on your jacket there."

I sighed. He and I left the food trailer, stepping into the shade of the surrounding buildings. This part of town had been a residential neighbourhood with a nice commercial strip, bulldozed to make room for enormous new condos popping up all over the place. This particular patch was one of the last holdouts—areas closer to downtown got hit harder by greedy developers, who took advantage of the post-rebellion damage to snatch up cheap property. This neighbourhood was far enough out it managed to avoid all that. Even these landowners couldn't resist the gigantic amount of money the condo developers must have offered.

Ever since structural engineering advances began allowing for taller buildings, each plot of land had become much more valuable. Holdouts saw larger and larger suitcases full of cash pushed in their faces.

Everybody has a price, I guess.

Besides, I doubt this patch had seen any sunshine in at least a couple of years, after all the other buildings shot up. Any it had was second hand from the glass-covered skyscrapers around us, so it must not have been a particularly nice spot to run a business or live in a house anymore.

We were about halfway done putting together the skeleton—the 74th floor—but there was still a lot of work to do. It would hardly be the tallest in the neighbourhood, but far larger than the old condos along the Lakeshore or in Liberty Village. At least, the ones that hadn't been torn down because a developer wanted to build something taller or they were condemned from the shoddy handiwork that was so common back when I was a kid.

The new guy and I walked over to a handful of the crew chatting around a pile of material, catching the tail end of Gael wildly gesturing.

"...they landed yesterday and brought 15 tons of pure gold back with 'em," he said. "Landed at the airstrip in Yellowknife. Yellowknife, of all places! You're the captain of a spaceship, you can land anywhere on Earth you want, and you choose the Northwest Territories. Can you imagine how much it's going to cost them to ship 15 tonnes of gold from there to the US?"

"They could sell it here," said Leopold, taking a drag of his cigarette. "There's a market for gold in Canada too." He held up his left hand and pointed to the wedding band on his ring finger.

"True," Noble reached down his shirt and pulled out his own gold necklace.

"I thought you said your parents got you that necklace on a trip to Italy," said Leopold.

"Oh yeah, I guess they did," said Noble. "Good memory."

"People buy gold here, yeah" said Gael, "but there aren't any facilities in Yellowknife that can process it. They'd still have to ship it here or to Calgary or something."

"Yeah, and they use gold for computers and shit mostly," said the new guy. "Most of it is probably going to China or some shit."

The crew and the buildings towered over me. I'm pretty sure I was the shortest thing in the neighbourhood, other than fire hydrants or patio chairs or mailboxes or garbage cans or planter boxes or something. Okay I guess I was taller than some things, but certainly the shortest living thing, except maybe dogs or cats or squirrels or raccoons or pigeons.

"That's the first time someone's come back from Mars, right?" asked Leopold.

"Alive, yeah," said Gael. "There was that one trip they messed up a few years back though, remember?"

"Yeah, what was that ship called again?"

"The Mary Celestial, I think" said Mateah. "That landed in Yellowknife too, didn't it? Did anyone figure out what happened?"

Like the rest of the crew, Mateah towered over me. My eyes came up to about her neck, which made it hard not to trace my gaze right down her chest, but I made a valiant effort. She and I took the same subway route, and I ran into her pretty often in the mornings. Why couldn't it have been her on the train, instead of that bloody Ignatius guy?

"I heard all the fuckin' air leaked out and they suffocated," said the new guy.

"No, it was a patch of radiation in space," said Karter.

"Yeah, that's what I heard too." Avery adjusted his hard hat—a poor fit over his turban.

"You guys are such sheep. They purposely set it up to fail," Draven sat hunched on his perch atop a pile of steel beams. "They didn't want us to find the evidence of—"

"Says here they're still investigating it," Keith looked up from what might be the last iPhone left in existence. I can't believe he gets service for that thing anymore. "I guess they brought it back remotely and stored it at a base in Johannesburg."

"Bunch of sheep," Draven muttered as he sat back down, shaking his head.

"Still? It was a decade ago!" said Karter.

"Yeah, well you try investigating something that happened a million miles away in space," said Gael.

"Shouldn't be that hard to figure out if there was an air leak or something," said Avery. "Just, like, stick it under water and look for bubbles or something."

"I'm sure they thought of that," said Gael. "They're a lot smarter than you are."

"Hey, screw you man," Avery shoved Gael into me and nearly knocked me over. "You're an idiot too."

"Never said I wasn't," Gael grinned, shoving Avery back, "but I'm a genius compared to you."

Avery slammed into Eddie, who had just arrived.

"Holy hell Avery," Eddie stumbled backward, staying vertical only as a result of his stocky frame. He pushed his shaggy hair out of his face. "Gaining a little weight there? Feels like I just got hit by a truck."

"Oh piss off," said Avery.

"Anyway, whatever you were talking about is boring," Eddie waved his hand, before I had a chance to ask why they'd bother moving the ship from Yellowknife to Johannesburg, almost literally the other side of the world. After all, there must have been somewhere closer. "Check this out, I heard about it this morning, it's way cooler. So there's this guy, right? And he's got this disease where his muscles are all weak and stuff so he can't walk good or do nothin' good, so they built him this wild exoskeleton suit that lets him walk and move around again, right?"

"You think that's not boring? They've been doing that for years now. Big deal."

"Shut the fuck up Mateah, you didn't let me finish. So anyway, this guy's in this exoskeleton thing right? And it's designed to let you walk but he can't run so good. But this guy was a marathon runner before he got the disease and he starts learning how to push his exoskeleton with what's left of his muscles. He ends up running the Toronto Marathon. Wild, right?"

"Bullshit. They don't let people with cybernetics in regular sports," said Brynlee. His heavy beard and thick eyebrows made him look angrier than he probably was.

"Yeah, the article talked about that. They made an exception for him because the exoskeleton makes it harder for him, not easier."

"Maybe there's hope for you then," said the new guy, jabbing a good-natured elbow into Karter's side. "Though I bet you could run a dozen marathons without breaking a sweat with those things," he motioning to Karter's legs.

Karter snapped from jovial to bitter in a heartbeat, slapping the new guy's arm away and shoving him into me, knocking us both to the ground.

Why am I always the collateral damage?

"Fuck you man. You think it's fun to lose your legs?"

"Whoa, take it easy Karter. I'm sure he didn't mean nothin' by it," said Eddie.

"Well maybe Gill here should keep his mouth shut about things he doesn't understand."

Gill, right. That's his name.

"Come on," said Mateah as she put her hand on Karter's shoulder. Karter slapped it away without looking.

"You can jump higher and run faster though man, how the fuck is that bad?" Gill asked as Eddie helped him to his feet. Meanwhile, Draven helped me to mine.

"What did I just say?" Karter shouted in Gill's face. "You deaf or something? How about I saw off your legs and see how you like it? You want to see how awesome phantom limb pain is? You want to see how cool it is to have to take your legs off when you're trying to hook up with some chick?"

Poor guy. It happened about a year and a half ago. There was a piece of plywood covering a hole in the floor of a building we were working on. Karter stepped on it, the wood splintered, and he fell down several stories. They tried to save his legs, but I guess they were too badly broken. He'd only been back for a few months—I guess it takes a while to re-learn how to walk.

After meeting Karter's gaze for a moment, Gill looked downward. "Well fuck man, sorry I upset you, I didn't mean it."

Karter grunted an unacknowledged acknowledgement.

I looked down at my boots and kicked a clump of grey dirt off the toe of my left foot. The clump came off but it left a mark behind, an island of grey against the ocean of blue rubber, shaped a little like South America.

White scuff marks crisscrossed the boot and lapped against the 'coast'. I kicked at it, an act of God which eroded land and flattened mountains. Most of the southern part of the continent had been obliterated, falling into the ocean in a cataclysmic event, the likes of which had never been seen. Researchers into plate tectonics were baffled as to how they failed to predict such a monumental catastrophe, and had begun consulting with fringe theorists to redraw their own theories.

"So what do you guys think this meeting is about?" Noble cracked open the icy silence.

"Byron didn't say much. I'm sure it's boring administrative bullshit as usual," said Avery.

"Probably," said Mateah. "Or maybe he's telling us our next job is on one of those 200 storey buildings they're making now. Have you guys seen those?"

"There's no way that's what this meeting is about," said Gael. "It's going to be a nice chance to take a nap and that's it."

"Don't be so sure," Sam arrived in time to respond, along with Kay, a carpenter on our crew who also happened to be his next door neighbour. I was always happy when she arrived, mainly because she was the only person on the crew other than Eddie who didn't make me feel horrendously minuscule. That, and I had a bit of a crush on her. She looked a lot like my first crush back in high school—short, with long curly black hair usually pulled back in a bun, and she was an artist.

I've always had a thing for artists.

Oh, and Sam. As the assistant foreman for the crew, he was the only guy other than Byron who knew what was going on.

He wore the same clothes he'd worn every day I'd seen him for the last fifteen years: a long sleeve white t-shirt, sleeves rolled up, underneath a pair of sand coloured overalls. His hair was getting longer though; the beginnings of a greying afro peeked out from under his hard hat that made his head seem rounder than it already was. "This one's going to be interesting."

"Sam, hey!" said Eddie. "I thought I heard Lucy coming in, haven't heard her in a while."

Lucy was Sam's 2028 Corvette Z06. One of the last cars ever made to run on fossil fuel, or so Sam told us. It was by far the loudest, smelliest, most obnoxious car I'd ever seen in my life.

Were all cars like that back in the day? I couldn't imagine living in a city like that. Barely anyone bothers owning cars, since it's so much easier to take an aloocab or the maglev, and even the people who do have electric ones. Well, except Sam, I guess.

"Yeah, it's hard to find fuel these days for her. I ordered a tank a few months ago, and it arrived yesterday. It's only going to last me a few weeks though. I wish I could drive her more often."

"Why don't you retrofit it to run on a battery like every other fuckin' car out there?" asked Gill. " What's so great about gas?"

"Oh boy, here we go," said Kay.

"Have you ever ridden in a car that runs on an internal combustion engine?" asked Sam.

"A what?"

"A gas-powered car, Gill."

"Oh, no. I never even saw one before Lucy."

"Then let me give you a ride home at the end of the day today. You'll understand then. To rip out Lucy's engine is to rip out her soul."

"He's not wrong," said Kay. "It's overrated, I think, but it's still a unique experience."

"Thank god there aren't too many of those things around anymore," said Mateah.

"Yeah yeah, I know," said Sam. "When everyone was driving them it was bad news, but now there's only about three thousand of us gas-powered old farts around, so it's no big deal."

"That's an oddly specific number," said Kay. "How do you know that?"

"We're part of a community. Guys all around the world send in photos and videos of them in their rides."

"Guys?" asked Mateah.

"Well yeah, it's mostly guys," said Sam. "There are a few women in there too though."

"Got any change?" I turned around to see a bundle of discoloured rags approach the group. Atop the bundle was a dirty red toque, which framed a cratered and cragged face, skin and beard wet with sweat. This man was far overdressed for this warm April day. "Spare change?"

"Bugger off," said Eddie. "Get the hell out of here."

"Geez Eddie, you don't have to be so harsh," said Avery as the beggar shuffled away.

"I don't care. Got no time for lazy losers. If he wants some money he should get a job."

"The poor guy probably has a hard life anyway," said Mateah. "No need to make it worse."

"Yeah," said Brynlee, "what if he's a war vet and has like, what's that thing called that war vets get when they come home and think they're still in combat?"

"Yeah, it's an acronym. Starts with P. PCOS, I think," said Noble.

"It's definitely not PCOS," said Kay.

"No excuses. Got no time for lazy losers," Eddie repeated. "And no trespassers on the job site. I don't care if he has PCOS or whatever. We can't let these wastes of space start wandering around here. We can't let them feel like they're welcome here. Once one of them smells a free ride, we'll have dozens of 'em crawling around like cockroaches."

"Eddie's right," said Sam. "Company policy is to remove any trespassers from the premises by any means lawful and necessary. But they're right too, Eddie, you could be a little nicer about it."

"Aye aye, commander," said Eddie, snapping a mock salute.

"So uh, what was this meeting supposed to be about again?" asked Noble.

"Yeah, you said it was supposed to be exciting today," Gael said to Sam. "I don't believe it. Every meeting we've ever had has been boring as hell." The rest of the crew nodded along with Gael.

"Not this one," said Sam. "Byron and I have been working on it for a while. It'll be good, trust me."

"Gael's right, man." Eddie puffed himself up to look as large and husky as his shorter frame allowed and strutted around with an air of false importance. "Hey guys, so we got some numbers to go over here, huff huff, looks like we used 7.3 more bolts this week compared to last year on average, we need to keep our numbers down, head office is a-breathin' down muh neck, huff huff," he said to a chorus of chuckles.

"I know it's usually like that," said Sam with a grin, "but all I'm saying is you guys won't be bored this time."

"C'mon, give us a hint man," said Gill.

"Patience," said Sam. "You'll get nothing out of me until the meeting."

At 8 our group shuffled over to Byron's office trailer to join the rest of the crew. Byron was standing beside a matte black wooden box large enough for two people to comfortably have a picnic in. On the side was a familiar looking golden emblem—an arrow-pierced apple enclosed by a thin round gear, drawn like a stroke from an ink brush.

I knew I'd seen it somewhere before.

The lid of the box had been pried open, suspended a few centimetres above the box by the nails that once held it in place. I and a few others took a seat on piles of material, boxes, or whatever else happened to be around. The rest were content to stand.

"Hey, do you know where that logo on the box is from?" I asked Avery.

"No, but I think I seen it before."

Byron heaved his hefty bulk up beside the box and fiddled with that old tablet he's had for as long as I can remember. None of us could believe it still worked. Who uses tablets anymore?

"Mornin' everyone," said Byron. "I've got a big surprise for you today. You're all going to like this one, especially you Eddie."

"Oh good, you finally realized what a great worker I am and decided to give me a raise." Eddie said as he reclined on a pyramid of ducts, head resting on his hands.

"You're the laziest bum on Earth," said a noticeably disguised voice from somewhere in the group, not unlike someone in the midst of puberty who sucked the helium out of a balloon.

"Who said that?" Eddie said, leaping to his feet, nearly sending the ducts tumbling over. "Who the fuck said that?"

He scanned the crowd like an animal looking for his prey.

I rolled my eyes, and a few others snickered.

Eddie was a talented carpenter but he was the biggest slacker I had ever met. On any given day, Eddie'd do maybe two or three hours of actual work. The rest of the time he'd be taking an extended lunch break, or going on a coffee run, or talking to someone about nothing at all. At least, that's what everyone else told me.

Up in the crane, it was hard to tell, so I took their word for it. Somehow, though, he didn't notice. He thought he was one of the hardest working guys on the crew. Eddie did a good job of training the new guys, though, which no one else seemed to want to do, so Byron put up with him and his idiosyncrasies. Besides, his coffee runs were a nice break from the sludge that came out of the food printer.

"Alright Eddie, sit down," Byron said with the authority of a school teacher. Eddie, the class clown, reluctantly agreed. "Seems the guys at head office got a few new ideas for how to do things around here. Inside this box is somethin' that's going to make all our lives easier."

He pushed the lid off and I caught a glimpse. Or at least I tried; the sun reflected off a nearby building onto whatever was in the box, straight into my eyes. As the burn hole in my retinas receded, I saw a metallic, vaguely human-shaped figure arise slowly and deliberately from within, reaching its full height of eight feet or so. The taller it grew, the brighter it became, burning another hole in my vision. This one a luminous X shape.

As my vision cleared, I saw it was from the two bands of reflective paint across its boxy torso like one of those old-school safety vests no one wears anymore. Above that sat a flat trapezoid-shaped head, and on its sides hung four rigid, motionless arms. In between the bands, a collection of yellow-tinged solar panels covered the upper half of its body. On its head were two dark, narrow eye slits. And the same emblem from the box was emblazoned on the shoulder of its upper-left arm like a tattoo.

"Everyone, meet Hank. Hank is our new automated labour unit. Y'know, an aloo. The company keeps calling 'em ayy ell yews, but I ain't never heard nobody call it that before. Now let's see here. There's a thing I'm supposed to read to youse," he flipped through his antique tablet.

"Here it is." He cleared his throat. "The HNK-series from Eris Industries is the third series of android-type automated labour units spe... spefic-ically designed for high-rise construction environments," he read robotically. "Programmed to respond to voice commands and...ex...exta... exta-prolate? Extaprolate new tasks accurately based on previously programmed AI knowledge, the HNK series is fully prepared to meet all your carpentry and construction needs. Each main limb features 17... at... Atricu...lated... mani... manipli... manipliators? and a direct drive kime... kime...natic... ah the hell with it," Byron dropped his arm to the side and his tablet along with it. "The point is Hank here is yer new co-worker. It's going to be workin' with you to start, Eddie. Head office says it's already set up to do carpentry, so yer going to be spendin' yer time over the next couple weeks watchin' it to see if it's workin' right, just like you would with a new guy, only he's already better than you. I'm sure you all got lots of questions about Hank, so go ahead and ask 'em."

We'd all heard of aloos before. Hell, an aloo drove me to work. An aloo would have made me a hot dog too if I'd realized there was a meeting today. I stood in line behind an aloo last night when I was at the grocery store, no doubt on an errand for its owner since aloos have no need for zucchinis and mushrooms and ibuprofen and flavour packs for a more modern, less hideous food printer. Once I got to the front of the line I paid an aloo for my groceries.

Those aloos were different. Its imposing stature was like a skyscraper in the middle of a suburban neighbourhood. No, it was more like a skyscraper-sized bulldozer in the same neighbourhood.

Even if it didn't mean us any harm, it looked like it could make short work of every single one of us without breaking a sweat, or busting a gasket, or whatever it is aloos do when they exert themselves.

"How much can it lift?" someone asked after a moment or two of silence. I didn't notice whom.

"Uh, let's see here..." Byron flipped through the manual on his tablet. "Here it is. It's cleared for 500 kilogram loads. He can do 800 if we upgrade him."

"Why's it got four arms?"

"Two of 'em are for grabbin' and carryin' stuff, and the other two are so it can attach different tools like a drill or a saw or whatever, so it don't need no hand held tools. It's got a fifth arm too that comes out of its chest to keep it stable when it needs it. We can upgrade it with more if we need it."

"How's it get its power?" asked Mateah.

"It's got a big battery on its back. Runs 18 hours a day. It's kind of hard to see but it's got solar panels in between the reflective vest on it too that'll let him run 22 hours if it's a sunny day. When the battery starts to get low it knows to use the rest of its juice to find an outlet and plug itself in to recharge. It'll make you lot of bums look real bad."

"Does it have, like, a brain or whatever?"

"Yeah, sort of. It'll answer yer questions and recognize yer voice, and it knows its name. You can tell it to grab somethin', lift somethin', frame a door, tighten bolts, and a bunch of other stuff. It'll go do it too, but then it'll come back and ask you what to do next. It'll say good mornin', ask about yer weekend, yadda yadda, but it don't actually care about the answer. We can upgrade 'em to be smarter but head office told me it's never going to be true artificial intelligence, whatever that means."

"Can it operate the crane?" I asked.

"No, not this one. I asked about that but I guess they're still puttin' the finishing touches on the crane operating one. I guess operating the crane is harder work than bein' a carpenter," Byron said to a few chuckles from the rest of the crew. "Same goes with the backhoe and the excavator, Keith, so don't bother askin'."

I figured programming a crane operating aloo would be easier than a carpentry aloo. It would just be like one of those carnival games where you grab a stuffed animal with a crane, except with an aloo brain, right? Then again, what do I know about building robots?

"What about HVAC?"

"Yeah it can do that too, and welding and masonry and everything else but the crane and backhoe, but we're going to start it with carpentry."

"Are they going to send more of them?" asked Kay.

"Hank here is a test run, the first aloo ever to work on an Edcon job site. The company guys want to see how good he works. We might get a full team of Hanks or we might ship it back for a refund. We'll see."

"It has a kill switch built in, right?"

"I knew you'd ask somethin' like that Draven. Yeah it's got a kill switch, don't worry. The government's not going to tell it to start brainwashin' us, ya nut," Byron said to a few snickers from the crew.

"Does it have, like, feelings or whatever?"

"No, it's just a machine. You can be an asshole to it and it don't got the smarts to care. But uh, you probably shouldn't."

"Why not?"

"You lookin' for an excuse to be an asshole, Gael? You never needed one before." Byron responded, as the chorus of chortles arose once again. "I don't know, no real reason. Just seems like a good idea to not be an asshole is all."

"What happens if it breaks down?" asked Noble.

"Eris has a squad of maintenance aloos that wander around the city checking up on all the aloos they got runnin'. They stop in once every few weeks for maintenance, makin' sure their joints are all greased, update the software, and all that. But if they actually do break down, y'know, full-on stop workin', we can put in an order for the maintenance bots to take it to a repair depot. The guy from Eris said all I gotta do is call him, and they'd be here within the hour. We can buy our own maintenance bots too if we want, but the company ain't going to spring for that until they know whether Hank here is gonna work good."

"Yeah but what happens if the maintenance aloo breaks down?"

"I don't know Noble, yer askin' too many weird questions. Do I look like a robot scientist or whatever? They probably send a guy to fix it, I don't know. Ain't my problem."

"Can we watch it?"

"Yeah, I thought youse all would want to. Let me get through the rest of this stuff and we'll have half an hour or so to watch Hank in action. So it seems we've gone slightly over budget on a couple of things here and head office wants me to cover 'em with ya."

I looked at my phone to check the time.

8:07.

# 3

The next twenty-three minutes consisted of a number of sounds in the general form of Byron's voice, none of which inspired a single thought in my mind. I'm sure everyone else felt the same way. He may as well have been speaking Urdu. To a penguin.

Once he was done, we formed a circle around Hank. Byron inserted a triangular key into a lock on its back, opening a square panel.

"Just a minute here guys," he looked at his tablet and fumbled with the buttons and switches inside Hank's panel. "There we go. Hank, good morning!"

Nothing.

"The hell? Alright, hang on a sec here." He flipped through the manual and fumbled some more.

"Isn't it on already?" asked Noble. "It just stood up out of the box."

"It's got some hydraulic thing in its legs," said Sam. "Or pneumatic, electronic, or whatever, I don't know. Anyway it sits down when you put pressure on top of it, and stands back up when you take the pressure away. But other than that, no, we have to switch it on."

"Probably pneumatic," said Mateah. "Definitely not electronic."

"Is that it? That must be it. Hank, good morning! No? What the hell? Mateah, come take a look at this would ya? I can't never figure this stuff out."

"Why do you think I know how to work an aloo?"

"I heard you talkin' about programming and stuff before. And youse an electrician, ain't ya?"

"I mean yeah, but fixing robots isn't my job."

"It ain't none of these other bums's jobs neither," said Byron. "But you was just talkin' like you know what's what, so I trust you more than them. Take a look, would ya?"

After a moment, Hank's eye-slots lit up yellow and its joints loosened up with a subtle shrug. "There we go, good job Mateah."

"All I did was flick the on switch," Mateah muttered as she walked back to the group.

"Well whatever, it worked. Hank, good morning!"

"GOOD MORNING BYRON. GOOD TO SEE YOU AGAIN." Its head swivelled in Byron's direction in a smooth, horizontal motion like a record on one of those antique turntables dad used to insist sounds better than digital music. Because it had no neck, the best it could do was fix its gaze above Byron. It peered off into the distance like the captain of a ship struggling to cut through the thick fog he and his crew have found themselves in.

Its voice was deep, silky, and authoritative. A bit intimidating, but mostly pleasant. It sounded realistic enough, but the words flowed so rhythmically it was almost hypnotizing. Still, it was like hearing a recorded voice over a crisp set of speakers. No matter how good the speakers are, it still doesn't have the timbre of a human voice from a human throat.

"There we go. Nice to see you too, Hank. Hank and I—"

"THANK YOU, BYRON. DID YOU SLEEP WELL LAST NIGHT?"

"Err, yeah great, thanks. I forgot to mention, whenever you say his name he thinks yer talkin' to him so he responds. And if ya don't say his name he won't listen to ya. Anyway, we already met so it knows me. Sam too, he helped me set it up. But youse guys all gotta introduce yourself to it so it knows all of ya too. Go ahead Eddie, you go first."

"Okay. So uh, what do I do here Byron?"

"You just introduce yerself, same way you do with any new guy. Just make sure ya say his name so he knows yer talkin' to him."

"Okay. Salutations, my dear Hank!"

"HELLO."

"Greetings to you, fine sir! Lord Duke Edwin Robert Hallstrom the third, esquire, at your service," he said with a terrible fake English accent and an exaggerated bow. "You may refer to me as Lord Hallstrom The Magnificent." He stuck out his hand to shake.

"NICE TO MEET YOU, LORD HALLSTROM THE MAGNIFICENT. ARE YOU A LORD FROM ENGLAND?" Hank responded, swivelling its head in Eddie's direction but missing his handshake cue. Probably for the best—Hank's hands looked like they could easily have crushed any human hand, or a hand made of steel for that matter.

"Indubitably, fine sir Hank!" said Eddie.

"IS YOUR TITLE AN HONORARY ONE, LORD HALLSTROM THE MAGNIFICENT?"

"It is, Hank, but mine isn't," said Gael. "I am God himself, and you will address me as such."

"C'mon you two, quit bein' asses," said Byron.

"Alright, alright. I was just kidding Hank. You can call me Eddie. I'm from Utah. Ever heard of it?"

"UTAH MUST BE A NICE PLACE TO LIVE, OTHERWISE IT WOULD NOT HAVE A POPULATION OF TWO MILLION, THREE HUNDRED EIGHTY-FOUR THOUSAND, NINE HUNDRED AND SIXTY-FOUR PEOPLE. HOWEVER, I AM GLAD YOU LIVE IN TORONTO NOW, OTHERWISE WE WOULD NOT HAVE MET. I AM EXCITED TO START WORKING AT MY NEW JOB. AM I WORKING WITH YOU TODAY?"

"Yeah Hank, but first my friends here want to meet you."

"I LOOK FORWARD TO MEETING YOUR FRIENDS. PLEASE INSTRUCT THEM TO INTRODUCE THEMSELVES."

"Alright, uh, I guess you go next Draven."

"I'm not introducing myself to this damn thing. I don't trust it."

"Draven, come on man," said Gael. "What's the harm in it knowing your name?"

"I'm in enough government databases as it is. No way. It ain't happening."

"We can talk about this more later but can ya just cooperate this once? We got work to do here," said Byron.

"Not a chance. Later to you usually means never."

"Alright look Draven," said Byron. "This is going to happen whether you like it or not. And you telling it yer name don't make a damn bit of a difference. It already knows yer name, it just don't recognize yer voice. So either you introduce yerself now, or I record ya talkin' when yer not paying attention and get Mateah to program it into Hank herself. Either way Hank's going to know yer name and yer voice, but one way is going to make us real cranky, ya hear?"

Mateah sighed, and Draven glared at Byron for a long moment, weighing his options.

"The only way yer gettin' outta this is if you quit right now, or if ya take one of them vows of silence," said Byron.

Draven let out a long sigh. "Alright, fine, but if this thing ends up wiping all our memories or giving us cancer, that's on you." He turned to Hank. "Hi Hank, I'm Draven Garcia," he said with a scowl.

"NICE TO MEET YOU DRAVEN. WHAT IS YOUR JOB?"

"I'm a carpenter Hank, and I don't like you."

"I AM SORRY YOU FEEL THAT WAY DRAVEN. I HOPE YOU WILL CHANGE YOUR MIND."

"Don't count on it."

"Alright Gael, you go next," said Byron.

"Hi Hank, my name is Jiminy Cricket."

"Damn it Gael, cut it out."

One by one we introduced ourselves to Hank. Hank in turn gave each of us a pleasant greeting and asked a question or two. I was last in line.

"Hi Hank, I'm Auden Black."

"NICE TO MEET YOU AUDEN. WHAT IS YOUR JOB?"

"I'm the crane operator, Hank. You won't be seeing much of me."

"WHAT A SHAME. YOU SEEM LIKE A GOOD PERSON."

It's programmed to say that, I'm sure. I bet it would tell Jeffrey Dahmer or Mitchell Wilfred they seemed like a good person. Still, a little flattery is always nice, even when you know it's manufactured. I guess that's why they programmed it this way.

"Alright, you bums want to see Hank do his thing? Let's go. Eddie, Hank's going to be workin' with you to start. Go ahead and show him what he needs to do. Just pick up where ya left off yesterday." Byron said after the introductions were over.

"Okay boss. Hank, follow me."

"OKAY EDDIE. I WILL FOLLOW YOU. PLEASE LEAD THE WAY."

We all headed up to the third floor. Eddie went first, with Hank behind. I couldn't help but notice the way our new aloo friend walked. On the flat ground, it had enough room to accommodate its long stride, so it looked natural enough, but in the confined environment of the stairs, he was stuck. Even though he could easily have skipped two or three steps in each stride, Hank took them one at a time. His flat, boxy feet landed in the exact spot on each new step as he twinkled up the staircase. That couldn't have been comfortable, but since aloos don't have any feeling in their legs, or anywhere else for that matter, I'm sure comfort isn't something that crosses Hank's mind, or its processor, or whatever it is it uses to make decisions.

"Wait, how's it going to fit through the door?" asked Karter, who was behind me on the stairs. Before I could answer, Hank's legs retreated inside his torso, lowering him to the ground. He then turned sideways and rolled through the door on a set of wheels it must have had on the bottom of its feet. Once it cleared the door, it returned to its full height.

"Alright, let's see here," said Eddie once we'd all assembled. He took a look at the floor plan. "So we need to put up some walls and frame some doors today. So uh, what do I do with this thing?"

"Just tell him what you want him to do, same way you would with any new guy," said Byron.

"But I have to teach the new guys how to do it. They don't know how we do it here. I don't have to teach him, right? He already knows what to do?"

"Yeah he knows how to work man. It ain't as hard as you think. Look, check this out. Hank, tell Eddie about yourself."

"OKAY BYRON, I WILL TELL EDDIE ABOUT MYSELF. I AM AN ERIS INDUSTRIES HNK SERIES EIGHT ZERO FIVE THREE MODEL AYY ELL YEW, RUNNING AYY ELL YEW OS VERSION NINE POINT TWO THREE POINT FIVE SEVEN. MY COMPONENTS WERE BUILT ON VARIOUS DATES IN LOS ANGELES, SINGAPORE, TOKYO, AND BANGALORE, ASSEMBLED IN LOS ANGELES ON DECEMBER THIRTEENTH, 2052, AND SHIPPED TO THE ERIS INDUSTRIES HEADQUARTERS IN MONTREAL ON JANUARY TWENTY THIRD, 2053 WHERE I UNDERWENT A THOROUGH ASSESSMENT OF MY CAPABILITIES. I WAS

CLEARED FOR SERVICE ON MARCH TWELFTH, 2053. I WAS THEN ASSIGNED TO THE CONSTRUCTION FIRM EDCON AND DEPLOYED TO THIS WORK SITE ON TODAY'S DATE, APRIL NINTH, 2053. I AM PROGRAMMED TO RESPOND TO VOICE COMMANDS. I AM PROGRAMMED TO PERFORM MOST DUTIES ON A HIGH-RISE CONSTRUCTION SITE SUCH AS THE ONE AT WHICH WE ARE CURRENTLY LOCATED. I AM READY FOR YOUR COMMANDS. FOR FURTHER DETAILS PLEASE CONSULT THE ACCOMPANYING MANUAL. ADDITIONAL COPIES OF THE MANUAL ARE AVAILABLE ON THE ERIS INDUSTRIES WEBSITE AT H-T-T-P-S COLON SLASH SLASH W-W-W PERIOD E-R-I-S-I-N-D-U-S-T-R-I-E-S PERIOD C-O-N-S-T-R-U-C-T-I-O-N SLASH M-A-N-U-A-L SLASH M-O-D-E-L SLASH A-L-U SLASH H-N-K SLASH NINE SLASH TWO THREE SLASH FIVE. FOR TECHNICAL SUPPORT, PLEASE CONTACT ERIS INDUSTRIES TOLL FREE AT ONE EIGHT NINE FOUR THREE FOUR TWO THREE TWO SIX TWO EXTENSION FIVE EIGHT TWO SEVEN OR EMAIL SUPPORT PERIOD H-N-K AT E-R-I-S-I-N-D-U-S-T-R-I-E-S PERIOD C-O-N-S-T-R-U-C-T-I-O-N."

Eddie blinked. "Uh, alright. Did that make sense to any of you? I still don't really know what to do here."

"Treat him like a carpenter, Eddie, just tell it what to do," said Byron. "Here, let me do it first. Let's start with somethin' simple. Hank, frame that door."

"OKAY BYRON. I WILL FRAME THE DOOR FOR YOU. PLEASE INSTRUCT ME ON THE MATERIALS I SHOULD USE."

"Hank, there's a pile of aluminum beams over there. Use that."

"OKAY BYRON. I WILL FRAME THE DOOR FOR YOU USING THE DESIGNATED ALUMINUM BEAMS. PLEASE INSTRUCT ME ON THE NATURE OF THE ALUMINUM. HAS IT ALREADY BEEN CUT TO SIZE?"

"No Hank, you gotta cut it too."

"OKAY BYRON. PLEASE INFORM ME OF THE SIZE OF THIS DOOR. IS IT A STANDARD SIZED DOOR?"

"Yes, Hank. Eighty inches by thirty-six."

"OKAY BYRON. I WILL FRAME THE DOOR FOR YOU. PLEASE WAIT."

A hatch outside Hank's thighs opened to reveal a pair of sockets into which he plugged his lower arms. He raised them to reveal two attached tools: a circular saw and a nail gun. At the same time, he picked up two of the pieces of aluminum with his upper arms, brought them up to his waist, and cut them into exactly the right size. He placed each piece into position and nailed them in place with the nail gun.

What was most remarkable wasn't the speed with which Hank managed to complete this task—though that was in itself remarkable. It took Hank less than a minute, when Draven, the best carpenter on the crew, would have taken at least fifteen. It wasn't the precision either—though this too was impressive. Each piece was perfectly cut to fit together, each new nail a precise distance apart. No, what amazed me was the grace, the fluidity. Like a tai chi master on Adderall, Hank's entire being was devoted to the task.

No hiccups, no stopping to measure, to catch its breath, to think about the fight with his spouse, the death of a family member, job security, or how he couldn't wait for the weekend. No stress, no frustration, nothing but single-minded focus and efficiency, from pile of material to completed door frame.

"OKAY BYRON. I HAVE FRAMED THE DOOR FOR YOU. PLEASE INSTRUCT ME FURTHER."

"Ya get it now?" Byron asked Eddie, who stood dumbfounded while the rest of the crew muttered their amazement.

"Yeah, yeah, I think so," he said after a moment.

"Alright, give him his next orders."

"Okay. Hank!"

"YES EDDIE?"

"We need to build a wall frame right here." He looked up from the floor plan and pointed at the floor. "Use the same stuff you used for the door frame."

"OKAY EDDIE. PLEASE INSTRUCT ME ON THE NATURE OF THIS WALL. IS IT A LOAD BEARING WALL?"

"No Hank, just a partition."

"OKAY EDDIE. DOES THIS WALL HAVE ANY DOORS OR WINDOWS?"

"No Hank, it's just a plain old interior wall."

"OKAY EDDIE. I WILL BUILD THE WALL FOR YOU. PLEASE WAIT."

Hank began its second task with the same focus, the same quiet competency; a different set of patterns in which the master was no less practiced. Its limbs, moving in every direction at once and each seemingly with a mind of its own gave

Hank the grace of an octopus. In contrast with its metallic yellow finish and boxy design, Hank became both an imitation and a mockery of the natural world. It finished building the wall from scratch in the time it took the food printer to make my sandwich.

"Wow. Uh, we're making pretty good time here Byron," said Eddie. "I guess we can keep building up these units? But we're going to need some more material. Auden, you want to head up to the crane and bring us some?"

"No need for now," said Byron. "Just get Hank to bring some up. Don't worry Auden; Hank ain't replacin' ya here. But yer not going to get as much of a chance to see Hank do his thing as the rest of us so ya may as well soak it up now. Besides, Hank can carry it."

I shrugged.

"Okay. Hank, go get some more aluminum beams," said Eddie.

"OKAY EDDIE. PLEASE INSTRUCT ME AS TO THE LOCATION OF THE ALUMINUM BEAMS YOU HAVE REQUESTED."

"Hank, it's on the ground at the base of the building beside the steel beams."

"OKAY EDDIE. PLEASE INSTRUCT ME HOW MUCH ALUMINUM I SHOULD GET."

"Shit, I don't know Hank. As much as you can carry."

"OKAY EDDIE. I WILL CARRY FIVE HUNDRED KILOGRAMS OF ALUMINUM TO THIS FLOOR."

"Is that too much? That seems like too much. Hank, I guess bring, uh, three hundred kilograms?"

"OKAY EDDIE. I WILL CARRY THREE HUNDRED KILOGRAMS OF ALUMINUM TO THIS FLOOR," Hank said as he walked down the half-finished stairs.

I looked back down at my boots. What's left of the South America-shaped stain was still there. I imagined the tidal waves returning just as the remaining nations of South America had begun to return to some form of stability, this time striking the northeast part of the continent.

Venezuela, Colombia, and Ecuador had completely disappeared, and only a tiny corner of Peru was left—the highest-ranking government official a deputy mayor of a minor city near the Chilean border.

While the UN declared a state of global emergency, conspiracy theorists declared these floods as proof of a government-controlled weather machine used to cover up the evidence of corruption and abuses perpetrated by US-backed regimes. More refugees flooded the borders of what was left of Brazil and Bolivia, where they found a vast, unending rainforest to navigate before they came anywhere near civilization. Only a few made it to the relative safety of cities.

"Hold on a sec," said Byron. "Somethin' don't look right there. Let me see that plan." He studied it for a moment, comparing the work Hank had just done with what was mapped out before him. "I think that wall is in the wrong spot. C'mere, take a look."

"I think you're right," said Eddie. He grabbed a tape measure and checked the space. "Yep, it's off by three feet exactly. I guess I should have shown Hank the plan, huh?"

Three feet exactly. Even when Hank made a mistake he was precise with it. After a few moments, Hank returned with an enormous pile of aluminum beams in its arms and placed them in a neat pile.

"Hank, the wall you just built is in the wrong spot. We need to move it three feet to the left. Can you do that?"

"YES, EDDIE, I CAN," said Hank. We waited for him to take action, but he stood perfectly motionless.

"...Okay Hank, then yank out the nails and move it."

"OKAY EDDIE, BUT I DO NOT UNDERSTAND."

"Yank out the nails and move it Hank."

"OKAY EDDIE, BUT I DO NOT UNDERSTAND."

"Hank, what don't you understand?"

"I DO NOT UNDERSTAND 'yank out the nails and move it'," said Hank, repeating Eddie's phrase with a recording of what Eddie said.

"That goddamn thing is recording us!" shouted Draven. "Mark my words, we're all going to the death camps, and that's on you Byron!"

"Shut up, Draven," said Eddie. "What's the deal here, Byron?"

"I don't know," said Byron. "Maybe point to each nail and get him to yank 'em out?"

"Okay yeah, good idea. Hank!"

"YES, EDDIE?"

"See this nail right here?"

"YES, EDDIE."

"I want you to yank that nail out."

"OKAY EDDIE, BUT I DO NOT UNDERSTAND."

"What the hell, Hank? What don't you understand?"

"I DO NOT UNDERSTAND 'I want you to yank that nail out.'"

"Byron, what's the deal? Is it broken?"

"It should be fine. Try saying it more clearer like."

"Okay. Hank."

"YES, EDDIE?"

"Yank. This. Nail. Out."

"OKAY EDDIE, BUT I DO NOT UNDERSTAND."

"Stupid piece of shit!" Eddie yelled, kicking Hank in the leg. Hank responded to this abuse in the same manner a refrigerator would.

"Calm down Eddie, let me take a look," Byron said. He unlocked the panel on Hank's back and spent the next few minutes comparing it with the manual in his tablet. "Mateah, c'mere again would ya?"

The people of South America in my mind deserved a reprieve, so I turned to Sam. "Didn't you guys test this thing first?" I asked.

"Yeah of course we did. I mean, we didn't test out everything, but we turned it on and talked to it and it worked fine. This was supposed to be the full test run today."

"Yeah, if it doesn't know how to yank out a nail what good is it?" said Noble beside me.

"Everything looks good," said Byron. "I don't get it."

"Hank, do a self-diagnostic," said Sam. "I remember reading about that in the manual."

"OKAY SAM. I WILL DO A SELF-DIAGNOSTIC. IT WILL BE COMPLETED IN APPROXIMATELY TWO HOURS, FORTY-THREE MINUTES. I WILL INFORM YOU UPON ITS COMPLETION."

"You're not doing a fucking self-diagnostic Hank, we don't have time for that!" Eddie shouted, gesturing at the misplaced partition. "Just pull the nails out of the frame and move it over, how hard is that?"

"OKAY EDDIE, I WILL PULL THE NAILS OUT OF THE FRAME AND MOVE IT OVER. WHERE SHOULD I MOVE IT?"

"Uh, three feet to the left Hank," said Eddie, mild confusion replacing his frustration.

"OKAY EDDIE, I WILL PULL THE NAILS OUT OF THE FRAME AND MOVE IT THREE FEET TO THE LEFT."

"Okay. What the hell just happened?" he asked, looking around for an answer.

"I don't know," Byron shrugged, "but I guess it's working now. Let's keep going and see if there's any other problems."

Eddie continued to point Hank at tasks to do, and he did them, thankfully without any other hiccups. By the time 9 o'clock hit, he'd done more work than anyone else would have done in an entire day, and far more accurately. And for the first time in as long as I could remember, I wasn't in a rush to get away from a staff meeting.

# 4

Have you ever climbed to the top of a crane?

Probably not, unless you're a crane operator. There aren't too many of those around these days though, are there? If you haven't, you really can't comprehend how high up they are. I mean sure, you may have stood on the balcony of a condo on the 150th floor. Maybe you did the edge walk around the CN Tower. You may have gone on dozens of airplane trips over the years. Maybe you even jumped out of one of those planes once. But it's not the same as climbing up a crane.

Standing at the bottom of the ladder, you look all the way up to the tiny cabin in the distance, so small you can eclipse it with your thumb at arm's length. You get a funny feeling in the pit of your stomach. It's the same feeling standing on the edge of a cliff or staring up at the massive roof of a sports arena; your knees go weak, you lose your balance, and your butthole puckers a little.

If it's your first time, you'll regain your composure and you'll take a deep breath. Then you'll take your first few steps up the ladder, or the stairs if you've got one of those luxury cranes. Hey, there's no problem, and hey, this isn't so bad, and hey, I can do this. You continue to climb, bolstered by your newfound sense of confidence. You feel great. You're conquering this fear. You can do anything!

This, however, does nothing to prepare you for the crane's swaying.

Every crane sways.

It's designed that way—that's one of the reasons a particularly strong gust of wind doesn't snap it in half, sending you to an expensive death. Flexible structures are less likely to break than rigid ones.

It's the same reason bridges are designed to bow a little under the weight of the dozens of transport trucks, aloo-cabs, and family sedans rolling over them. But take my word for it and read as many textbooks on the finer details of structural engineering as you'd like. They'll do little to reassure the instincts of your monkey brain screaming louder and louder with each step to get the hell off this thing.

If it's your first time, you'll look down at the Earth below, thinking it will relieve your anxiety.

Rookie mistake. This is why there's no comparison between climbing a crane and climbing the CN Tower. In the CN Tower, you're surrounded by a concrete structure which protects you from the reality check gravity would love to slap you with.

Falling while climbing the CN Tower's stairs will mean a slight trip at best, or a tumble down a flight of stairs at worst. Sore knees or a sprained ankle, whatever. There's no realistic way you, being at the top of the CN Tower, could fall all the way back down to the solid ground without the actual building falling apart.

This is the case with the ladder too. The harness you wear protects you as well as the CN Tower's concrete cocoon. Like a car's seatbelt, it's designed to allow you to move, but catches at any quick jerk.

But your brain doesn't consider this when you look down and realize you're only about a third of the way up, and you feel a sharpness in the depths of your stomach. The hairs on your arms stand at attention like quivering stalagmites.

And it's still a long way down, even if you've only climbed a third of the way up.

Fear will hold you in place for a few moments. You're safe where you are, your monkey brain reasons, so you stay still. But you can't stay there forever. You've only got two options. So maybe you do give up, and climb back down, and go talk to your guidance counsellor, and switch to culinary school instead.

But maybe you're committed to becoming a crane operator, or you're too stubborn to give up in the face of a little fear, or you hate cooking.

So you climb up, and cling to the railing on the balcony around the cabin, and relish having some sort of solid ground that isn't the rung of a ladder under your feet, even if it is a few hundred feet in the air.

At the end of the day, if it's the first time, hey, you made it through climbing up, so climbing back down can't be as bad, can it? After all, you've been up there in the crane cabin all day and the height feels normal now, so it must be easier. Every step you take brings you closer to the ground when you climb down, right?

So every step becomes easier than the last.

Secure in your newfound logic, you open the cabin door and step out onto the balcony, prepared to start climbing down the ladder.

And that's when your monkey brain wakes back up and decides to give up yelling.

It grabs you by the throat with both hands and holds you in place. Your heart pounds against your ribs with the furor of a drummer in a death metal band. Legs and arms lock into place and secure you to the railing like a frozen corpse at the peak of Mt. Everest. This lasts for several minutes before you can build up the courage to thaw your limbs and climb back down. There's no shame in this; every crane operator has dealt with it their first time in the sky.

At least, that's what I told myself.

And you do have to climb back down, no matter how much you try to bargain with the situation. You're safe, but you can't stay here forever. You'll get hungry and thirsty, and eventually you'll have to use the washroom.

No, they're not going to send a helicopter to bring you back down. The price of hiring the helicopter is more than you could ever afford on a crane operator's salary, which you're obviously not going to get at this point, and the public embarrassment is going to be too much to handle.

No, the fire department isn't going to come bring you down. Even if their ladders were long enough, you still have to climb down their ladder in the first place. May as well save everyone the trouble and climb down the ladder you've already got.

Nobody is going to bring you a jetpack or a parachute either. You could get a hover drone to deliver one, but even if you did, wouldn't that be even more terrifying than climbing down the ladder in the first place?

Trust me, I've thought of everything. There are only three possible scenarios where you, having climbed to the top of the crane, would not have to climb back down: they perfect human teleportation technology (not likely anytime soon), the crane collapses altogether, or you jump. So no, you have no choice but to face that ladder. Your logical mind knows it. But you still need to convince your monkey brain. It gets easier, but it never really goes away.

It's instinct, programmed into your mind over millennia of natural selection. You can't unlearn it.

Sounds awful, right? So why do I love being in the crane so much?

Really, it's the view.

The gaggle of specks moving to and fro—it takes a moment before you realize these little spots are actually people, human beings going about their daily business. Are they black, white, men, women, something in between, gay, straight, cis, trans, rich, poor, friendly, mean? Who knows? Everyone is the same from up in the crane. The aloos are sometimes a little larger, and usually a little shinier, but that's about it.

You really get to know your city that way, too. No matter how tall they build the new buildings, your crane is taller. Otherwise, how can you bring everything to the top? At this site, at Dufferin and Eglinton, it gives a nice view of the areas yet to be bulldozed and developed, and the ones that gave way to the condos. They seem to cluster around the subway stops at first, and spread out along the main arteries like a buildup of cholesterol.

Bloor Street is almost entirely condos now, and so are St. Clair and Eglinton. If I was an alien looking at the city from outer space, I might think each street was built like a wall to keep people out, or in. My favourite view is the one south, and a bit west. High Park. They talked about bulldozing it to build condos for a little while, but I'm glad that never happened.

There are some condos built around the park, but I can still see Grenadier Pond on the south edge, and the people sitting in their boats—or the boats, at least, the people are too far away to see. I guess people are upset about all the condos being built, but now that they have aloos to plan out and dig new subway tunnels, people can get around more easily so it's not as big a deal.

I guess people still don't like that old buildings are getting torn down.

After 15 years of operating my crane, I could do everything on autopilot. Grab this stuff, bring it up to this floor, rinse, repeat. I knew that crane so well it became an extension of my arms. I mean sure, I needed to pay close enough attention to avoid hitting anyone or dropping the material I was moving or sending a pile of aluminum beams through a nearby window or swatting a wayward hover drone out of the sky, but that became second nature after a while.

That may sound boring, but there's more to it. In such a tall crane, you can see the entire city from one end to another. You can spot the up-and-coming neighbourhoods, see the rooftop gardens people built underneath the hypnotizing whirl of their building's wind turbines, and even chuckle at the occasional nude sunbather on their balcony.

When you're near the Lakeshore, you can see some of the larger buildings in St. Catharines and the northern shore of New York on the other side of the lake. But that's not the real draw of the crane.

That's not why I was always in such a rush to climb up to my cabin in the sky, and it's not why I hadn't taken a vacation in years.

When people go to space, they experience what they call the "overview effect".

Everyone who has ever been in orbit talked about it, from the earliest astronauts to the crews of modern ships. They feel blissful, connected to the whole Earth and everything on it, living and otherwise. A sense of "one-ness," as though they were connected to something deeper, grander, more important than the mundane problems of being late for work or paying the hydro bill or cleaning the autovac or running out of toothpaste that fill the minds of terrestrial people. Somehow, these things don't seem important when you can see how big everything is.

The Buddhists talk about a similar experience, but they get it after a few thousand hours of meditation, not from being in space. I've never been to space before, and I don't think I'd want to, but I got a taste of that feeling up in my crane. I enjoyed it so much I became antisocial, avoiding as many people as possible in the morning to head right up to the crane cabin.

No matter where I was or what I did, I was never more at peace than when I was in the sky.

# 5

"Man, that thing did it all today," Eddie said in between gulps from his pint.

At the end of the day, some of us would head to whatever local bar suited us best for a drink before heading home. Each time we started at a new job we'd check out a few different bars in the area to find something we liked. The criteria by which we judged a place were simple:

"I'll know it when I see it" was the only response Leopold could give when asked what a "good atmosphere" was. Most of us were content to find a spot with chairs and booze, whether a stylish modern spot, a grimy dive, or the same old boring sports bar your granddad used to hang out at. But this bar seemed to fit whatever it was Leopold knew when he saw it.

One of the more interesting things about our latest find, The Black Cat, was that it wasn't in a condo lobby, like every other bar in the area. It was one of the few buildings in the neighbourhood which hadn't yet been sold to a condo corporation. Made it feel like a bit of a time capsule, like the city's heritage buildings were evacuated during a natural disaster and somehow The Black Cat hadn't gotten the memo.

It wasn't the sort of place you'd go out of your way to visit—no Horseshoe Tavern or Buck Fifty Cafe. But if you were in the neighbourhood and you wanted an easy spot to grab a drink after a long day or to drown your sorrows, The Black Cat would do fine.

Arya, the bartender and owner of the place, stood behind the bar in the far corner of the deep, wide room, serving a few of the other regulars. If I had to guess, I'd say she was in her late twenties or early thirties, but it's rude to ask so I never bothered. Her long, wavy, multicoloured hair was one of the first things to notice when entering the place adorned by that understated brick or dark wood style that was so popular a few dozen years ago.

Well, that, and the flashing lights of the arcade machines in the corner. They were replicas designed by someone in the neighbourhood and placed in The Black Cat as a display. I guess you could buy them if you wanted, though it seemed the sort of thing that would be more fun to play in a bar than your living room. They only difference seemed to be they accepted payment via phone tap as well as quarters. I'm pretty sure they didn't have phone tap payments back when these games first hit the public.

She had three of them—Pac Man, Donkey Kong, and some other game called Burrito Blitz I think was designed by the same person who built the cabinet.

"The usual, folks?" Arya asked us as we walked in. We agreed, and most of us made our way to our usual table. Gael made straight for the dance floor with Leopold in tow, and Brynlee gravitated to the Pac-Man machine as though his hand and the joystick were both magnetized. The guys would talk about the same sort of stuff they talked about in the morning before staff meetings or at lunch. I wasn't particularly interested in any of it, regardless of the time of day, but if I didn't go they'd think me antisocial (which I was) or rude (which I was not), so I made sure to put in my time.

Besides, Arya had one of my favourite wines, so I didn't complain. But today it was different. We didn't have to hear Leopold complaining about his husband again or Draven telling us about the latest conspiracy theory he read on the internet.

"You should have seen it! 'Hank, lift this.' He did it. 'Hank, put it over there.' He did it. 'Hank, grab me a coffee.' He fucking did it. Man, he did anything I told him to, and never even bothered asking why or complaining. He carried big steel beams and concrete blocks and shit like they weren't nothin', and he framed an entire floor's worth of walls before the morning was done. He'd have wiped my ass too if I asked him, and he'd probably thank me after."

"Yeah, we saw it this morning," said Avery. "Piece of junk barely worked. You had to tell it a hundred times to yank the nails out before it caught on."

"No no, we figured that out man," said Eddie. "It's the stupidest thing but that was all because it didn't know the word 'yank.' You have to use really basic words when you're talking to it."

"It doesn't know the word 'yank'?" asked Avery. "Seriously? Who built that thing? How much more basic can you get than 'yank'?"

"I don't know man, some nerds in a science lab or something. They don't think like we do. I bet none of them has ever done any actual work in their life. Bunch of lazy losers, you know? They might not know the word yank, but I bet they got lots of experience in yanking, if you know what I mean?" He stroked an imaginary dick in the air and, as if his intention weren't obvious enough, added some sound effects.

"I can't believe that was the issue," Mateah did her best to ignore Eddie. "That's ridiculous. Seems like an amateur move to not program casual language into a robot built to work in a casual language atmosphere."

"Isn't it hooked up to the internet?" asked Noble. "You'd think it could look up what any word means."

"I don't know man, what do I look like, a fuckin'...goddamn...uh, robot builder? What do you even call someone who builds robots anyway?"

"A robot...ologist?" suggested Avery.

"Nah that can't be it, that doesn't sound right," said Noble. "Robotician?"

"Robotician?" said Avery. "That sounds even worse than robotologist. Makes you sound like a mortician. Maybe a robotician deals with dead robots, like, finds out how they died or something."

"Do robots die?" I asked.

"I don't know," said Avery. "You have to be alive before you can die. Are robots alive?"

"Probably not," said Noble, "but like, you can still find out how it died, right? Or stop working, whatever. That's the point of a mortician, right? Maybe that's what a robotician does too."

"Too deep for me, boys," said Eddie. "You sound like my good for nothing cousin, just sits around all day talking about philosophy and junk. Waste of time, you ask me. There's work to be done."

"The word you're looking for is robotics engineer," said Mateah.

"Oh yeah, that makes sense," said Noble.

"I don't fucking buy it yet," said the new guy. Shit, what was his name again? G- something, I think. Greg, Gary, Gulliver... "How can a robot do everything a human can do? It can lift more, but it's got no fucking brain, man. It's only as useful as the guy telling it what to do. We saw that this morning."

"Whatever Gill, you're jealous Hank's a better student than you are," said Eddie with a good-natured elbow jab to the ribs.

Gill. Gill. Gill.

"He's got a point," said Keith. "We can tell it to do stuff, but what happens when the stuff is done? It doesn't know what to do next like we do. It can't think. It's just a tool."

"I'm sure it'll be able to figure it out," said Mateah. "If they can build a robot to do all your jobs so perfectly, I'm sure they can build a robot that can read blueprints."

"It's gonna be able to do your job too," said Eddie. "You're not that special."

"That'll be the day," said Mateah. "One wrong move and the robot's gonna electrocute itself. Then poof, there goes the company's million dollar investment, or however much those things cost, and then they'll have to spend another million to call me in to fix the problem."

"Same goes for you," said Eddie. "Remember that time you almost fried yourself at the Eglinton job?"

"I don't know what you're talking about," said Mateah. "I've never made a mistake before. You must be referring to the guy who came before me."

"That's you, shithead," said Karter. "Back when you were a guy or whatever."

"There's no evidence of that," said Mateah. "Mateah Eccleston has a completely flawless record, go ahead, look it up. You goofs can't even tell the difference between me and another electrician who's not even the same gender as me? Maybe Arya should stop serving you. I think that booze is killing too many brain cells."

"But aren't you—" Noble began.

"She's messing with us, doofus," said Avery.

"Oh, yeah, of course," said Noble. "I knew that."

"Shit, did you see that?" shouted Eddie, bouncing back and forth between Gill and Draven to either side of him like a player getting a high score in a pinball game. He gestured to the baseball game on the wall-mounted TV across the room. "The bases are loaded and Lee-Roye Henderson is up to bat. This is going to be huge." He pushed his chair back a little bit, prepared to celebrate the big move, or play, or whatever it's called.

"Yeah, but look, Min Yee is pitching," said Kay. "He's the best in the league."

"And Henderson is the best batter."

"So either way, this should be good," said Mateah.

"Are you cheering for the Dodgers over the Jays?" asked Eddie, feigning offense. "I'm deeply crushed."

"Oh who cares, it's not like any of them are actually from Toronto. A game's a game, but there aren't any hometown heroes there."

"Not true, Min Yee is from Toronto."

"Yeah, and he's playing for the Dodgers, so really, I'm the one cheering for the home team. You're just cheering for a logo."

"Anyway, Hank is working way faster than any of us," Noble ignored the game and tried to change the subject from the joke he'd missed, not realizing that had already been done for him. "You saw how quickly it framed that door. A handful of those things could easily replace all of us carpenters, and the welders and HVAC guys too. Even you, Mateah, superstar electrician. Then a couple more to operate the heavy stuff," he gestured to Keith, "and your crane," he gestured to me, "and the company needs only one guy to tell them all what to do. We're all done here."

"Done is right. Those things are going to be the death of us," said Draven. "Do you know how much radiation they give off? Do you know how toxic the paint they use is? If we spend too much time near those things we're going to get cancer. It's all part of their plan, man. They want to reduce the world's population to make us easier to control so they use those goddamn things to make us all sick and take our jobs." The chalice of black beer he drank, combined with his black trench coat he always insisted on wearing outside the job site even in such warm weather, made his statements seem even more menacing and absurd.

"Come on, Draven, that's fucking crazy," said Gill. (I remembered!)

"Is it? Do some research kid; look up 'aloo paint toxic'—you'll find the truth. It's so obvious and you sheeple live with your heads in the clouds."

"Don't argue with Draven, Gill," said Eddie. "He's done his research."

"You're damn right I've done my research. I've done my research on what the plan is with that HNK model. Did you know it was originally designed for the military? That's why it has such a bulky body—half of it's made of layers of shielding. That thing was designed to withstand bullets, bombs, lasers, you name it. I bet they didn't even get rid of the code that allows it to kill people. Stay in line, or we'll shoot you dead, that's the message they're trying to send with those things."

"Damn!" shouted Eddie. "Henderson struck out. I can't believe it; how could you fuck up that badly? Unbelievable."

"New high score, bitches!" said Brynlee as he returned to the table. "I am invincible! The Pac-sterminator!" He mocked a pose of heroic triumph, standing right below one of the pot lights on the ceiling. Its light glistened off the part of his bald head that wasn't covered by the bandanna he'd tied around it, adding to the effect.

"The Pac-sterminator?" asked Gael, having returned around the same time. "That's the dumbest thing I've ever heard."

"Oh piss off, Gael. You're just jealous you can't handle these skills," said Brynlee, waving his fingers in the air as though he was playing an invisible piano or casting a spell.

"Yep, you're right," said Gael. "I'm jealous that you spend all your time getting the high score on an antique video game. Are you still a virgin or what?"

"You're such a dick," said Brynlee.

"Do you think you could beat Hank at Pac-Man?" asked Noble.

"Totally, I'd kick his ass no problem," said Brynlee.

"Does Hank even know how to play Pac-Man?" asked Avery. "I think his hands would be too big to use the joystick."

"Forget his hands," said Gill. "How's he going to get through the fucking door?"

"He fit through the doors on the job site, didn't he?" said Keith. "I'm sure he could fit through this one too."

"Yeah, it was cool, he like, shrunk his legs down and rolled sideways through the doors," I said.

"Yeah, I'm pretty sure Hank can fit anywhere he needs to," said Brynlee. "But you're right Avery, his hands are too big to use the joystick. I guess that's one thing we humans will always be best at."

"Looks like your high score is safe for now, then," said Avery.

"I'm sure Hank could just plug directly into the arcade machine and get a high score that way," said Mateah.

"That wouldn't count," said Brynlee. "That's cheating."

"How would it be any different?" asked Avery. "It's the same thing, whether he's programmed to operate the joystick or programmed to plug right into the machine."

"It's like an AI chess program," said Mateah. "It's only as good as whoever programmed it. But if you're the Pac-Sterminator, no one is better than you, so I'm sure you'd win every time."

"You know it," said Brynlee, flexing his bicep.

"Yeah," said Eddie, coming out of his athletic revelry. "Hank is going to make all our days easier. Damn if he doesn't make mine easier so far, at least."

*Your day couldn't get much easier,* I thought, surprised to hear the same words out loud in Keith's voice.

"Oh fuck off Keith, what do you know about hard work, sitting in your little backhoe all day? Relaxing in your comfy chair like you're king of your fucking castle. Enjoying your air conditioned little cabin, sitting on your ass just pulling levers all day. Don't judge me, you've got it easier than any of us do."

With the last sentence, he swung his arm across the crew in a clumsy gesture that knocked Draven's drink over toward Gael, who leapt to his feet a moment too late to escape the wave of ale flowing toward him.

"Eddie, you goof!" he yelled, gesturing to the area where his lap had been. "Looks like I pissed myself now!"

"Oh, man, you pissed yourself? Hey Arya," he called to the bartender, "could you grab a pair of fresh underwear for my friend Gael over here? He just pissed himself."

"Fuck you, Eddie!" Gael shouted, shoving him out of his chair.

"And another drink for Draven too!" said Eddie from the bar floor, raising his pint in the air, of which he'd somehow managed to avoid spilling a single drop. Arya smiled and shook her head as she brought a drink and a cloth over to the table.

"Anyway, all I'm saying is I'm looking forward to more Hanks," said Eddie as he climbed back onto his chair. "The more the better."

"Yeah, and we'll all get bottom lined," said Draven, sipping his new pint.

"Draven you're nuts man, that ain't going to happen," said Eddie. "Byron wouldn't do that to us. Even if head office wanted it he'd fight for us. Byron's always had our back. He's the best guy I've ever worked for. He's not going to take away our purpose."

"I can't believe I'm about to say this," said Brynlee, "but Draven is right. Why would the company buy a squad of aloos to do all our work for us and keep us on the job site? It doesn't make any sense. There's no reason to pay us."

"I'm telling you Byron's not going to let us get bottom lined. Plain and simple. You don't know Byron like I know him, man. He cares more about us than any other guy I've ever worked for. He's going to make sure we've all still got jobs, I know it."

Brynlee began to respond. "Come on Eddie—"

"Enough. It's not going to happen. I ain't never going to be one of those good-for-nothing bottom line losers. End. Of. Story."

## 6

The next morning ran much more smoothly than the last, thank god. But while I remembered my maglev pass, I'd forgotten my book, so I turned to the well-read newspaper I found resting on a seat in the maglev. The cover story caught my eye so I opened it up and read some more.

In what is being hailed as one of the greatest medical and scientific breakthroughs in human history, surgeons at Johns Hopkins University in Baltimore, Maryland, have successfully performed a brain transplant between two human beings.

The patients, who asked to be identified only by their first names, Victoria and Evan, were placed in a medically induced coma before the 106-hour procedure. Doctors will keep them in that state for the next week to monitor for complications.

So far, though, everything looks good.

"This is a breakthrough of unprecedented magnitude, said Dr. Phineas Celsus, the team's, ahem, head surgeon. "Both patients are stable, and we're optimistic they will be able to resume living healthy, productive lives following their recovery."

Celsus assembled a team of thirty-seven surgeons, advisors, and assistants for this monumental task, which was completed yesterday morning.

As I read the article, I found myself as amazed by the scientific miracle as I was by this newspaper existing in the first place. After all, everybody I knew got their news online. While I never really read the news, when I did it was on the internet too, or on the window of an aloo-cab, though that wasn't terribly frequent. But the shuffled and disorganized state of this paper told me at least one other person read it. The fact increased the readership count to at least two, and if two people cared, there were probably a few more.

What are the odds the only two people who still care about newspapers in the entire world happened to live in the same city and get on the same maglev on the same day and the first person happened to leave the paper in the exact spot it needed to be for me to have happened upon it?

And if only two people cared, wouldn't they print two copies of the newspaper? Or even one copy and send it to the first person with instructions to forward it to the second person when they were done? Or not even bother with the whole thing in the first place, what's the point of operating the printing press and paying all the journalists and editors and photographers and everyone else if they were printing two newspapers a day?

There were probably aloos for most of those jobs now, but you'd have to worry about the property tax on your building downtown and all the things you'd need to run a newspaper, which I can't think of because I've never run one.

The ads in this paper were for so many kinds of things that would appeal to so many people odds are most of these companies wouldn't sell a single product if there were only two readers. Like the Scarlatto, a machine designed to apply makeup. I guess it paints your face according to specs. The part where your face goes looks like the mask a serial killer would wear in one of those old-fashioned horror movies.

"Your sexiest self in seconds". I could see that being a useful tool for someone who likes to wear makeup.

Or for this one—a surgical treatment to grow longer eyelashes.

"Enhance your beauty, naturally," the ad told me. I wasn't sure how a surgical enhancement could be considered natural, but what do I know about this stuff?

Not that I'm judging—people can do whatever they want, and I definitely appreciate a beautiful, made up woman as much as the next straight guy.

These ads aren't exactly my thing, so unless the other person who read this paper is a feminine type with a bunch of disposable income and an obsession with beauty, these advertisers are advertising to no one at all—if there really are only two people who read the paper, which is sounding unlikely. And even if whomever it is that reads it is the type of person these ads will appeal to, buying ad space for one person still wouldn't be worth the money when they could go with internet ads or holograms in Dundas Square or those annoying subway ads or show up and sell the products to them.

There were advertisements for personal food printers, aloo assistants, those horrible Snappy Cake things, new cars, plastic surgery, LifeSim, recruitment for class-action lawsuits against a couple of the condo development companies and the perennial ads for escorts of all shapes and sizes that have taken up the last dozen pages for as long as I can remember.

I wasn't even an avid reader of the newspaper, since I picked it up off the seat on a whim, because I forgot my book.

Two seats over, a woman buried in one as well. With her blonde hair pulled back into a high bun, her grey skirt and matching grey blazer atop a white blouse, and her confident, poised demeanour, she looked like the stereotype of the young corporate executive in stock photos on advertisements for lawyers and real estate agents, even though barely anybody works in those jobs since most of them were bottom lined years ago.

Her paper was open to the financial section—she must be some sort of banker or executive. One of the few they haven't gotten around to replacing yet. She must be important. Or maybe she's a model for one of those stock photos and she's headed to a photo shoot, and she's reading the financial section because she's trying to get into character, though they probably have the clothes for the models at the site of the shoot, so they don't get all wrinkled and messed up as the model travels.

You really can't tell the difference between computer-generated images and reality, so why would they bother paying models when they could digitally animate one and no one would ever know the difference?

A guy in red sweat pants and a windbreaker stood a couple rows away reading a paper too. Based on his outfit and physique, he looked like he was on his way either to or from the gym. Probably to—he wasn't very sweaty, though I guess he could have showered. His paper was open to the comics and games page, which had a crossword puzzle, one of those chess puzzles, and some comic strips. He wasn't writing anything down, so either he was one of those super geniuses who could memorize the crossword, or he was enjoying a silly comic.

An older lady was reading too—*Pride and Prejudice*. God, I hated that book. I had to read it in school when I was doing my undergraduate degree, before I dropped out and became a crane operator. I didn't really know what I wanted to do after high school, but I knew I liked reading. So, why not study English literature? But after three years, I realized any joy I got from reading disappeared. So, I dropped out.

I don't remember the name of the book I was reading that brought me to that realization, but I do remember the main character was a crane operator. And I didn't have any better ideas for what to do with my life, so here we are.

But I don't regret it, even if it was a waste of money. The first time I read *The Iliad* was in school, and we were exposed to all sorts of other great works. The history and music theory electives I took were great too.

A handful of others were scattered throughout the maglev. A trio of crust punks carried big camping backpacks and funny haircuts, their clothes cobbled together with a series of monochrome patches printed with the logos of bands I've never heard of, likely as loud and obnoxious as the people who wore them. They were accompanied by a pair of brown mutts, maybe with some Labrador blood, but I don't know much about dogs so don't take my word for it. Their collars enveloped their necks in a series of spikes which provided more of a sense of intimidation than the two dogs, lying peacefully on the train's floor, seemed to be able to accomplish on their own.

A couple of guys with hard hats and lunch pails were doing their best to ignore the crust punks. I couldn't help but compare the two groups: both dressed in dirty, grimy old clothes that told the world they didn't care what they looked like, but one of the groups put a lot more effort into cultivating that image than the other.

Another man with a leather briefcase and black slacks sat a few seats away. Despite his closed eyes, his body was alert, his attention seemingly devoted to the pair of buds plugged into his ears. Like the banker/model lady, I found myself wondering where this man could have been going—maybe he was a model too.

Two seats down from him, a young, thin, scantily clad person slept, their crooked wig of bleach-blonde hair partially obscuring the dramatic makeup they wore. They must have been returning from a party the night before.

Maybe I should pass them this newspaper and show them the ads for the beauty treatments, because it seemed like the sort of thing this person might be interested in. That would probably be offensive or something though, because who wants a construction worker, or any stranger, really, to come up and tell them about the beauty treatments they should be getting, especially when they're sleeping and possibly still inebriated from the party they probably just left?

There was even a seated aloo, holding a newspaper open in front of it. Why an aloo would take the maglev to get anywhere when it could walk, I don't know. Maybe it was on an errand for its owner and had to fetch something on the other side of the city, or its battery was running low, or it was in a hurry, or its owner could barely afford an aloo, but didn't have enough money to afford for the aloo to take an aloo-cab. Why would it read a newspaper, since it could get information from the internet. There were definitely no stories or ads geared toward aloos in this paper, but that was probably for the same reason it was wearing clothes: stylish red corduroy pants and a denim jacket over a plain white t-shirt, a Toronto Blue Jays cap on its head and dark brown boots. At first glance I couldn't tell it was an aloo. It wasn't until I saw its face—kindly, but obviously artificial—that it became obvious. I'm sure it didn't need any of this stuff, but it seemed to make people feel more comfortable when aloos were clothed, especially with the increase of aloo sex workers. I wonder if sex workers collect bottom line cheques—ah, screw it.

The maglev used to be so full of people in the morning that if you managed to make room for yourself, you'd end up spending the ride in direct contact with a dozen strangers crammed up against your body so tight you couldn't even raise your arm to hold on to the pole and stabilize. Not that you needed to, of course—your human swaddle would keep you on your feet, whether you liked it or not. And would you be crammed up against a nice looking lady with sweet smelling perfume or floral shampoo, or a rambling drunk who'd pissed himself? Roll the dice and test your luck. That's after a previously successful dice roll that won you a spot on the train in the first place. Depending on the station and the time of day, you could expect to miss several trains before you got on.

Now the trains run precisely on schedule 24 hours a day, with robotic efficiency, unless someone jumps in front of them, which only happens a few times a week. And they managed that without having to drag the country into fascism.

Ironically, the trains started getting efficient around the same time people stopped relying on them as much. Thousands of octopuses must surely have given their lives for the amount of ink spilled by columnists noting the irony—if transit had worked this well before, the city would have run much more smoothly, and on a more personal level, I wouldn't have been late for my first job interview after I graduated. Things worked out well for me at Edcon, but still, I would have saved myself a lot of stress that day.

Overall the ride is nicer now, but there's one thing I miss about the old subways: the anonymity. No one would bother creating a mental catalog of their fellow riders like I did when they were drowning in a sea of heads and shoulders. You'd be another grain of sand on the beach, too common a sight to be noteworthy as anything other than one component of the larger whole.

And if there happened to be a particular tuna sandwich-eating, onion-spewing maniac onboard that you wanted to avoid, it would be a lot easier.

You could both be on the same car a dozen feet from each other and the human swaddle would protect you from being spotted. But when there are so few people on board, you may as well size them all up from your own little private corner of the maglev. And if there's someone on the train you didn't want to see, well that's too bad.

Not one of these people looked familiar, which was a relief. But each step off the train at Dufferin Station brought a new measure of fear to my heart, wary of another mustard-coated attack.

"Oh, hey Auden," I heard from behind me. My brief sense of panic dissipated once I realized it was Mateah's voice.

"Good morning, uh, I guess you were at the other end of the train, huh?"

"Yep. How do you feel this morning?"

"Just fine, I left after you did, and I only had one drink."

"That's good, I'm sure it's not a good idea to operate a crane while hung over. Hey, where are you going?" she asked as she walked toward the escalator.

"I really hate those weird ads, I'm going to take the other escalator."

"Okay, you go ahead. I think they're cool. I'll see you on the job site, I guess?"

"Yeah, see you there."

I stopped for a hot dog.

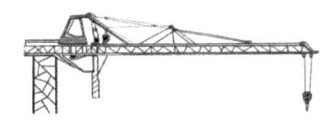

A gentle cacophony rumbled at the edge of my mind like waves lapping at the shore, pushing further with every step onto the site. When I arrived, I discovered the source of the sound: music coming from a stereo Eddie was playing. Byron let him play it so long as no one in the neighbourhood complained, and no one had yet—at least not on this particular job site.

```
"DID YOU NOT HEAR ME, AUDEN?"
```

I turned to see Hank approaching from the other side of the job site, closing several feet with each stride. The speed at which he walked, the aggression with which his arms swung, the sheer massiveness of his frame, and the reverberations I could feel through my feet all combined to scare the hell out of me.

"Oh, hi Hank. No, I didn't hear you," I swallowed my urge to turn around and flee in terror.

```
"I SAID: GOOD MORNING, AUDEN. DID YOU SLEEP WELL?"
```

"Yeah, thanks Hank."

```
"YOU ARE WELCOME, AUDEN. DID YOU WATCH THE BLUE
```

JAYS GAME LAST NIGHT?"

"No."

"IT WAS QUITE A MATCH. FAITH POTTER SCORED THREE HOME RUNS AND INCREASED HER BATTING AVERAGE TO DECIMAL THREE FOUR ZERO."

"Is that good?"

"YES, THAT IS GOOD. ALTHOUGH FAITH POTTER IS A ROOKIE, HER PERFORMANCE SO FAR HAS BEEN EXEMPLARY. I, AND MANY OTHERS, WILL BE WATCHING HER CAREER WITH GREAT INTEREST."

Exemplary? Who uses the word exemplary? And why does Hank know what exemplary means but not yank? And why does he think I care about baseball? Who the hell programmed this thing?

Before I had the chance to ask any of these questions – probably for the best; Hank wouldn't have had any of the answers anyway – Eddie stepped out of the food trailer with a sandwich in his hand, this one vibrant with pastel reds and yellows. They'd refilled the food colouring.

"Auden, hey man," he shouted as he walked toward me. His approach was not much less aggressive, though far less terrifying, than Hank's was. Probably because Eddie wasn't much taller than my five foot six (and a half!) instead of a machine nearly twice as tall as me that could tear me in two. "I've got Hank into baseball, cool huh? Did you watch the game last night?"

"No, but I was in the bar while you did."

"Oh yeah, I guess you were huh? Man, Faith Potter is unreal, I bet she's going to win rookie of the year. But hey, check this out, it's so cool. Hey Hank, what song is playing?"

"THIS IS THE SONG *UNWILLING GHOST* BY SWVM."

"I didn't teach him that, he just knows it. I guess he gets it from the internet or something. So cool!"

"Pretty amazing," It wasn't really, considering we've all had devices that could do that for decades now. But Eddie was excited about it, so why ruin his day?

*Unwilling Ghost* ended, and another song came on. "I bet he'll know this song too. Hank, what song is playing now?"

"THIS IS THE SONG UNBROKEN, *UNSHAVEN* BY THE BUDOS BAND."

"He knows the old shit too, cool!"

"I bet I can stump him," said Avery as he approached.

"Oh hey, good morning man. What's up?"

"Just a sec," said Avery. He turned off Eddie's stereo.

"Hey what the hell man!" Eddie shouted, smacking Avery on the shoulder. "I love that song!"

"Shut up and relax for a minute will ya? Put on your lab coat—we're going to do a little science experiment here. Hank, what's this song?" Avery began to sing *"movin' down to Chinatown, lookin' for the girl with the crooked frown."*

After a brief pause, Hank responded, "YOU ARE SINGING THE SONG ROBOT LOVER BY THE BELLY BUTTONS."

"Whoa, no shit," exclaimed Eddie. "He didn't even need to hear the real song. That's amazing!"

Hank must have taken the lyrics someone sang to it and done a quick search online. Or maybe it had some sort of pitch and rhythm recognition software, but then again Avery wasn't exactly the world's greatest singer. Either way, I'm sure the software wasn't that complicated. It was like these guys had never seen a computer before. But why could Hank look up the lyrics to a song, but not the word yank?

"That is amazing," said Eddie. "Hank, what's this song? *My spirit's young my heart is old, there's nothing to me but dust and bones.*"

"YOU ARE SINGING THE SONG KING OF REGRET BY—."

"Damn Eddie, you're a terrible singer," Avery interrupted.

"Hey, fuck you man, you're pretty terrible yourself."

"Better than you!"

*You're both pretty terrible,* I thought.

"Oh yeah? You think you're Knoxley Adams here?" said Eddie, at which point I realized I hadn't thought my last statement at all, but said it out loud.

"Uh, who's Knoxley Adams?" I fumbled.

"Damn Auden, do I have to spell it out to you? I'm telling you you're a shit singer too."

"Well yeah, heh," I said nervously. "That's why I became a crane operator, instead of, uh, a singer."

"Why don't you sing a song to Hank too, and then we'll ask him who he thinks is best," suggested Avery. "I'm sure he's got some way to tell the difference between you two hyenas and a golden-throated god like me," he said as he touched the front of his neck in a pose of statuesque virtuousness.

"Yeah, do it Auden," said Eddie.

This was a stupid waste of time. "Uh, I should get up to the crane."

"The crane will still be there in a minute," said Eddie. "Just sing a song."

"I don't know what to sing," I stammered, fumbling at the last excuse I could think of.

"Shit I don't know man, think of your favourite song. It's not that hard. Just sing something. Whatever pops into your head."

"Okay fine, if it'll make you happy," I said with far more confidence than I felt. "Hank, what's this song? *She makes plans like the rent is cheap, hailin' a cab from the patio seat.*"

"YOU ARE SINGING THE SONG THE GIRL FROM THE BEACHES BY MYLES ROGERS."

"Unbelievable Hank, you know everything," said Eddie.

"Hard to believe he could tell what either of you were singing," said Avery. "I'm surprised he didn't try to call the dog catcher or something."

"Shut up Avery," said Eddie. "Hank, who do you think is the best singer of us three?"

"I HAVE INSUFFICIENT CAPABILITY TO ANSWER THE QUESTION."

"Well Hank, what do you need to answer the question *sufficiently?*" Avery asked, giving air quotes to the last word.

"HNK UNITS ARE NOT EQUIPPED WITH MICROPHONES SENSITIVE ENOUGH TO PRODUCE SOUND RECORDINGS OF HIGH ENOUGH QUALITY TO ANSWER YOUR QUESTION. WE ARE DESIGNED TO UNDERSTAND AND ACCEPT CONVERSATIONAL REQUESTS WITHIN FRIENDLINESS PARAMETERS AS ESTABLISHED WITHIN WORK SITE BANTER PROTOCOLS, BUT NOT TO ANALYZE SOUND QUALITY. I REQUIRE A MORE SENSITIVE MICROPHONE IN ORDER TO PROPERLY ASCERTAIN THE QUALITY OF YOUR SINGING VOICES ACCORDING TO PITCH, CADENCE, TIMBRE, AND RHYTHM," said Hank, missing out on Avery's condescending tone. "I ALSO REQUIRE ADDITIONAL SOFTWARE TO ANALYZE SAID VOICES, WHICH IS NOT A STANDARD COMPLEMENT FOR THE HNK SERIES."

"Okay Hank, but based on the microphone and software you have, who do you think is the better singer?" asked Eddie.

"I HAVE INSUFFICIENT CAPABILITY TO ANSWER THE QUESTION."

I looked up at the crane.

"Well, Hank," said Eddie, "we're not going to get you a new microphone but what if we downloaded the software? Would you be able to tell then?"

"WITH THE REQUIRED SOFTWARE, I COULD PROVIDE AN ANALYSIS OF THE VOCAL RECORDINGS I HAVE JUST CREATED. HOWEVER, IT WOULD NOT BE SCIENTIFICALLY ACCURATE. THE ANSWER WOULD BE USEFUL ONLY FOR ANECDOTAL AND ENTERTAINMENT PURPOSES."

"Did you hear that?" asked Draven as he walked by. "I told you, that damn thing is recording every word we say. I'm not saying a word anywhere near it ever again, and I suggest you all do the same."

"Okay Draven, that's a good idea," said Eddie. Draven walked away, shaking his head. Eddie jabbed Avery in the ribs. "Anyway, looks like your little science experiment is kaput, Avery."

"Whatever. Hank, download the software," said Avery. "How long will it take?"

"TO DOWNLOAD AND INSTALL THE NECESSARY SOFTWARE AND PROCESS EACH OF YOUR VOICE SAMPLES WILL TAKE APPROXIMATELY ONE HOUR, THIRTEEN MINUTES, AND THIRTY-TWO SECONDS. YOUR ACCOUNT WILL BE DEBITED ONE HUNDRED FORTY-TWO DOLLARS AND THIRTY EIGHT CENTS."

"Okay Hank, do it," said Eddie. "I guess we'll find out later boys."

"Are you sure?" I asked. "Won't it get charged to the company or something? We might get in trouble"

"Yeah, it's fine," said Eddie. "Byron won't notice. And if he does, we'll just pay for it, split three ways. That's only, like, forty-five bucks each."

"Less than an hour's wages," said Avery. "Okay yeah, no big deal."

"Download the software and analyze the recordings you just made, Hank," said Eddie. "We'll know who won by lunch time."

"OKAY EDDIE."

"It's obviously going to be me," said Avery. By the time Eddie made whatever rebuttal he made, I was already three rungs up the crane's ladder.

# 7

So speaking, bright armed and far gazing, I lightly sprang, heart burning, and emboldened the Achaeans to gather, pushing onward to engage the Trojans. Bronze upon bronze set ablaze, shivering edges of shield and spear and plume, and brave Trojans lay at our feet, shattered and broken. Skyward their lifeless eyes turned, their final act of supplication to their patron god.

Ignophenes the swiftest of the noble Phrygians whom, through marital bond with King Priam's daughter, were honour bound to defend the noble city, was first to fall. Thundering forth, a flaming flash amidst the ranks of the Achaeans, he drove his spear, meeting only my own, which I drove into his chest, now pushing it forward, now pulling it back.

"Noble Ignophenes, surely Elysium bound, farewell" I cried. Then, to my fellow Achaeans, I raised my voice, "Be mindful of your might, warriors! Zeus has willed this day to our glory. Stand with me, and gather to deliver the fury of Zeus to the Trojans. They shall not stand against us, but rather shall we drive them to their walls this night."

So, with chariots and shielded warriors thronged about, soon had we gathered battalions in honour of unbreakable Ares or warlike Athena. Forward we pushed, and leapt the fiercer on our foes, setting our whole hearts to the battle, acting as one. As when a huntsman sets his hounds upon a wild boar, so upon the Trojans did we Achaeans set ourselves. Halios, Blanor, Callimakhos - these leaders of the Trojans we slew, and thereafter descended upon the multitude, and even as—

"Hey, I asked you a question Auden," said Sam. "Come on, snap out of it would ya?"

So, let me explain.

That was an astral projection. It's how I passed my time up in the crane. I know what you're probably thinking, but stay with me here.

Back when I was a kid, we had a "take your family to class day" or something. like that, where you brought somebody in to talk about whatever they wanted. One of the kids brought their weird hippie uncle to talk about astral projection. I don't remember his name, but I do remember the bright pink paisley cloak of a shirt he was wearing. Also, the long, tattered beard into which he had woven a few beads and braids, and the musky putrid smell I would later come to recognize as a blend of essential oils and body odour.

"Think of a place you've been before," he said to us as he hovered toward the front of the class, both arms outstretched as though he were Moses parting the Red Sea.

"It works best to choose a familiar place. Like your bedroom, think of that. Now, close your eyes and clear your mind. Imagine sitting on the corner of your bed, or at your desk, or standing in the doorway. It doesn't matter where. Focus on the lamp in your room—everyone has a lamp, right? Now here's the tricky part. Turn your head in the direction of the lamp where you are. For example, if you're sitting on the edge of your bed and your lamp is to your right, turn your head to the right as you imagine yourself looking at the lamp.

"Keep focusing," which I found oddly easy to do despite the distracting scent in the air, "And notice all the details of your lamp. What colour is it? Does it have a shade on top of it? If so, what colour is it? Is it made of wood, plastic, metal, or something else? How tall is it? Is it on your desk, or is it a floor lamp? Are there any scratches or chips in it? Have you put any stickers on it? If you don't know some of the details, don't worry. Your mind will fill in the gaps.

"Can you picture your lamp clearly now?" I went to nod my head yes. "Okay, good. Now allow your brain to fill in the gaps with what's in the area around that lamp—but keep your gaze focused on the lamp itself. Think of the surface it's on. Is it on your table? If so, what else is on the table with it? Is there a clock, or a book, a glass of water, a piggy bank, a teddy bear, a toy, a candle, a sculpture, a phone projector stand, or anything else on the table? What does the wall behind the table look like? Is it painted, or wallpapered? What colour is it? And what about the floor? Is it wood, tile, stone, concrete, plastic, carpet, or something else? Do you have a rug? If so, what colour is it? Does it have any designs on it? Is there maybe a window behind your lamp? If so, what can you see outside from where you're sitting?"

At this point, I had been perceiving my room almost as though I was actually there. All the different elements of it came into focus, piece by piece, until my entire field of vision was filled with my room. I was still looking at the lamp on my desk, but the rest of the room was clear. This is the point where it started to get really interesting.

"Now, turn your head, and imagine your gaze moves with it as clearly as if you were actually there. Allow the details of everything else around you to come into focus as you look around. Imagine the colour of the paint on the walls and ceiling, the colour of the floor, the light switch, the light itself, the blanket on your bed, the pattern on the blanket, the colour and shape of your bed frame, the colour of the area rug, the windows, the blinds on the windows, the cobwebs in the corner of the window, the view from the window, the toys strewn across the floor, the door to your closet, the view of the hallway outside your door, the old fashioned computer sitting on your desk, and on and on. Imagine every little detail you can think of and picture it in your mind as clearly as you can. Remember, it doesn't have to be perfectly identical to the way your room is, it just has to be clear in your mind. Allow your mind to fill in the blanks with whatever it comes up with – don't fight it.

"Can you see the room completely now? Good. Now continue to look around, and find a new anchor to focus your vision. A picture on the wall, a door, a piece of furniture, it doesn't matter. Allow your mind to reassemble the details of that area based on your new anchor. Now move your head in the other direction, and find another anchor over there.

"Sort of feels like you're there, doesn't it?" I agreed with this sentiment so wholeheartedly I was tempted to walk over to my bookshelf and grab a comic book to read.

"That's what we call astral projection. If you practice, you can use your imagination to travel anywhere you want."

And then I did, all day long while I sat up in my cabin in the sky.

"But what about the crane?" you might be thinking. "Isn't it hard to be sitting with your eyes closed while you operate a piece of heavy machinery like that?"

And yeah, you're right, but the guys on the ground couldn't use the material as fast as I could bring it up, so I spent as much time sitting and waiting as I did actually using the crane—often more.

It was lonely and isolating, and I never got a chance to talk to anyone—the same reasons I would later fall in love with it.

But when I first started operating the crane, I paid much closer attention to what I was doing. After all, I was fresh out of school and wanted to make a good impression on this crew I'd joined. So I took my orders, pulled the levers, and let the day pass by.

Once you've been doing something long enough, it becomes second nature. My cousin plays drums in a band, and she once told me when they were jamming out new tunes she'd start zoning out and thinking about anything but what she was doing. I guess it runs in the family. Anyway, after a few minutes or so she'd snap out of it and realize she hadn't lost rhythm or played anything stupid. I don't know if all musicians get this sort of thing, but I know crane operators do. Or at least this crane operator did. I'd been operating the crane for more than fifteen years and projecting since I was a kid.

I could envision myself in the cockpit of a World War II spitfire pulling back on the throttle while another part of my mind was paying close attention to the crane, pulling levers and moving things around as though I were giving it my undivided attention.

But what's really happening? The hippie who taught us this seemed to believe astral projection actually projects us through time and space, and if you have your spirit centred and your chakras aligned etc. Some even say you can get hurt or die while you're in the ethereal realm in the same way you can die in the corporeal realm. I don't buy any of that, but I don't think it matters anyway. It's a fun way to pass the time.

The guys thought me cold or distant or uninterested, and they weren't wrong. It's not that I had anything against any of them—I liked them all fine. Even Draven, who everyone thought was a weirdo. I mean, he was, but he wasn't a bad guy.

But all they did was talk about their mundane lives and complain about the same junk everyone else complains about. That couldn't compare with the lives I lived in the crane. Why would I care about things like the baseball game last night when I could escape and become a Greek warrior in the Trojan War? Or the skipper on a 17th century sailing ship? Or the lead guitarist in a band playing to a crowd of a hundred thousand people?

Besides, astral projection only really works when you have a clear mind. If not, all sorts of weird things can pop up.

I never mentioned what I did up in the crane to anyone, not even Sam who called up to me most often to give me instructions. How could I? Imagine how that would go down. Someone would ask me "how's life" or "what's new," and I'd say "oh fine thanks, I just led my army to victory over the Romans at Cannae, and later this afternoon I plan on piloting my star fighter through a battle with the Morgloks from the planet Vega VII."

No thanks.

In the interest of both avoiding the endless barrage of ball-busting that the guys would throw at me, and preserving my reputation as someone who wasn't completely bonkers, I kept the astral projecting to myself.

The only interruption I got in the crane was from Sam, and it was always jarring at first. One moment I'm leading an army, and the very next I'm yanked back to reality by a man whose voice bore as much resemblance to a baritone cicada as it did a human being.

Despite that, though, I did appreciate Sam checking in with me and chatting. It kept me from drifting too far off into my own head. If not for Sam, I'd probably have lost touch with reality altogether and moved to a monastery or signed up for the next mission to Mars.

I just wish he had a better way of doing it.

"Yo! Earth to Auden! You sleeping up there or something? Wake up buddy!"

"Oh, sorry. No, I'm awake, heh. What's up Sam?"

"You are!" he said with a chuckle. He'd been saying that same joke ever since we started working together fifteen years ago, and every day he said it with as much gusto as if he'd just come up with it. I don't think Sam will ever get tired of that one. "I said what do you make of Hank?"

"It doesn't make much of a difference from up here. He looks the same as the rest of you, only a bit shinier."

"Well yeah, but having him around period. You're no dummy. You've read what's going on. If things work out well, it's only a matter of time before we're all bottom lined."

"Is that so bad?"

"Depends on who you ask. Eddie loves complaining about bottom liners like they're too lazy to work or something, as though there were still enough jobs to go around. He sounds like one of those idiots my uncle used to listen to on those old-fashioned talk radio shows. I think it'd be alright. It would give me a chance to do what I've always wanted to do if I had the time."

"And what's that?"

"Take my family to Kenya and get in touch with our roots, of course."

"I didn't know you were from Kenya."

"Well I'm not, really. I was born right here in Toronto, but my grandparents came here in the 1980's. They'd be so disappointed if they knew I'd never taken their great grandkids back home. My cousin lives there and he came to visit once, and I always thought it sounded cool when he spoke in Kiswahili, but I never had the time to learn more than a few phrases here and there. I'd love to take my daughters there and introduce them to their heritage, and get to know my heritage a little better too."

"Have you ever been there before?"

"Yeah, a few times when I was a kid. I guess it's changed a lot since then. I have some family there who I haven't seen in years. My wife and I tried to arrange a trip a few times but it never seems to work out. Her parents are from Ethiopia, actually, which is north of Kenya so we could go visit her family too. I think it would be great for everyone. Have you ever been to Africa?"

"No, I've never travelled anywhere really. Just to Montreal with my parents once when I was a kid."

"Once we're bottom lined you'll have a chance to travel more if you want. I don't know if Kenya is the place for you, but it's a big world out there and you've only seen a little slice of it. Like Korea, I've always wanted to visit there too. The food they have down in Koreatown is some of my favourite in the city. I'd love to see how authentic it is. And they built a long highway there a few years after reunification with no speed limit like the old Autobahn in Germany. I'd love to take a drive on it. It would be hard getting Lucy over there, but I think it'd be worth it. Really give her a chance to roar, you know?"

"Yeah."

"What is it all those government ads say? 'The freedom to do whatever you want' and all that, clouds blowing past in the sky across lush green fields and beautiful people enjoying life."

"Something like that. But I guess not everyone thinks that way."

"Pretty much everyone does except Eddie."

"Yeah, I noticed. Why does he get so angry about bottom liners?"

"I don't know. It never made any sense to me either. Of all the people here, you'd think Eddie would want to be on the bottom line more than anyone else. The way that guy works, it's like showing up is enough for him to think he's earned his pay. I like Eddie, but it's obvious he's not a hard worker and he never will be. Why would a guy who clearly doesn't like hard work not want to take advantage of something like the bottom line? Why is he so condescending to people who've been bottom lined when he could choose to work harder but doesn't?"

"I don't know. Maybe he likes hanging out on the job site or something."

"He'd better get used to the idea. Hank seems to be doing good so far. Eddie does even less than he used to; now he sits around and tells Hank what to do. Before when he trained the new guys, at least he was hands on and helping show them how to do things. He does know his stuff. But he doesn't even try to look busy now. The other guys do, but they know what's up. They'll be bottom liners soon enough. We all will. Head office ordered two more aloos for the site—they'll be arriving here in a couple of weeks."

"Two more aloos?"

"This stays between you and me, but yeah, they're coming. As far as I know they're identical to Hank. Byron and I haven't gotten orders to let anyone go yet, but it's gotta be coming soon, right? If these two new aloos work out as well as Hank, that is. And I see no reason why they wouldn't if they're the same as Hank. So be prepared, that's all I'm saying."

Be prepared.

At least I had something to be prepared for other than the crushing uncertainty people dealt with back when jobs were being replaced with aloos on a regular basis with no solution for how people were going to make ends meet.

When the first few aloos hit the market, it wasn't so bad. They were expensive for the companies to deploy, and frustrating for their customers to use. Some of the bigger corporations actually invented the first aloos decades before they started using them, though I don't think they called them aloos back then.

The truth is it was cheaper to pay a few people a few bucks an hour than it was to buy a squad of robots and pay someone with the technical know-how to maintain them. But like all technologies, they got better, easier to produce, and cheaper. And as people got more expensive and robotics became cheaper, aloos became much more appealing.

My dad was in one of the first industries to be replaced.

He was a loan officer, and a pretty good one too, judging by the box full of old employee of the month plaques my mom and I found collecting dust in her storage unit a few years ago. But his job could easily be done by an aloo, so the company he worked for decided to let him and most of his colleagues go.

I looked into it just after we found those plaques. The aloo that replaced my dad was barely even an aloo by today's standards. It was just a piece of software, really, which they installed on my dad's old computer at his old desk. Certainly nowhere near as impressive as Hank, or even the aloo that makes hot dogs outside the maglev station. But it doesn't matter what it looks or sounds like or how impressive it is. If you have something that does the work you used to have to hire a human to do, you have an aloo.

Anyway, dad bounced around from job to job after that doing whatever he could find. He couldn't hold one down for more than a few months before he was replaced there too. He did some odd jobs and freelance work wherever he could for a while, but in the end it wasn't enough.

My mom had a stable job as a counsellor for people recovering from drug addictions, which she still does today since they haven't found a way to automate it yet. But her salary wasn't enough to keep our family afloat. We ended up having to sell our house and move into a small apartment to make ends meet.

We weren't the only family to face this problem. It started to get really bad around the beginning of the 2030s when I was a teenager. It's simple math, really. If there are 10 of a thing people need, and 15 people trying to get that thing, the result is at least 5 unhappy people. And if that thing is essential for someone to be able to take care of themselves and their family, you've got 5 desperate people. Maybe even 5 people willing to go to extreme measures.

Now imagine instead of 5 people, it's 10 million people. 10 million people across the country with no jobs, no prospects, nothing to lose, and nothing but spare time on their hands. There were protests, riots, and all sorts of other nasty business, both here in Canada and for the Americans down south. They blew up cars, burned down buildings, and even kidnapped a few members of parliament at one point, if I recall correctly.

Everything changed once the unionists started to get replaced. The union members didn't want to see their siblings suffer, so they arranged a system where a company still had to pay a replaced worker half their wages for the rest of their life, and the union itself would pay the other half. The workers would still be able to enjoy their lifestyle, and the company still saved money with an aloo.

Union dues for those who were still working skyrocketed as a result, but people seemed to be okay with it for a while at least.

Eventually the government took over and expanded the idea, calling their new program the "Bottom Line." As in, let's establish a bottom line for society and let's not let anyone fall below it. Good thing, too—the unions were going bankrupt trying to do it themselves. They had to raise taxes on businesses that used aloos to pay for it, but companies were still better off hiring an aloo than paying someone their full wage.

At least, that's what I've been told. I was only a kid at the time, so I don't remember any of it. I don't remember anything from that period other than typical kid stuff. And there's no physical evidence left. Part of establishing the Bottom Line program was the protesters rebuilding everything they damaged in their rebellion. Since they were all unemployed anyway, they were happy to do it.

I guess it speaks to how well my parents held things together despite it all. But stoic though he was, the stress and uncertainty of those years took its toll on my dad; he died of a heart attack two years after getting his first Bottom Line cheque, when I was ten years old.

"...don't you think Auden?"

"Yeah, uh, definitely, of course." Sam's question brought me back to the moment. He had the tendency to say in 50 words what the average person said in 5, so I figured I could pay attention about 10% of the time and still get the idea of what he was saying. And 90% of the time, I was right.

"Oh yeah, there was a reason I buzzed up to you there in the clouds too. They're ready to start welding on the 4th floor, and the guys there told me to tell you to start bringing their material up to them so they could get down to business. Anyway, I've talked your ear off already Auden, have fun up there!"

I heard a faint voice in the background.

"Oh, that was Eddie. He said Hank told him he's the best singer of the three of you. Whatever that means."

# 8

A few weeks later, our next two aloos arrived, this time without any fanfare. The rest of the crew had had enough of a chance to work with Hank from day to day that the excitement had worn off. I showed up to work that morning to find Hank standing in line with the two new guys. The three were completely identical, three soldiers from the Terracotta Army plucked from their museum complex where plenty more awaited deployment. Eddie stood in front of them, paintbrush in hand.

"Hey Auden, come over here man!" Eddie called to me. "Clint, Blake, this is Auden. He works here too." Each aloo's eyes lit up a different colour as Eddie said their name.

"NICE TO MEET YOU AUDEN. WHAT IS YOUR JOB?" the two machines said in unison. Both voices were identical to Hank's but in a different vpitch. They harmonized together perfectly in what sounded like a minor dyad, both sad and hopeful at the same time.

"I'm the crane operator. You won't be seeing much of me."

"WHAT A SHAME. YOU SEEM LIKE A GOOD PERSON," the robotic chorus responded.

"HE IS A GOOD PERSON," said Hank, his yellow eyes lighting up. "HE LIKES TO WATCH BASEBALL AND HE IS THE BEST SINGER ON THE CREW."

"You must be broken, Hank," said Eddie far too quickly. "You definitely said I was the best singer."

"I DETECT NO ABNORMALITIES IN MY MEMORY. HOWEVER, A DEEPER DIAGNOSTIC MAY REVEAL MORE SIGNIFICANT UNDERLYING ISSUES. SHOULD I RUN A DIAGNOSTIC?"

"No Hank, don't worry about it." Eddie was caught in the lie and he knew it. Besides, this wasn't exactly an issue of national security, was it? "Why does Hank think I love baseball?"

"EDDIE INFORMED ME THAT ALL CREW MEMBERS AT THE 720 DUFFERIN STREET JOB SITE ARE AVID AND ENTHUSIASTIC FANS OF BASEBALL."

"Yeah, I might have said that," Eddie said with a laugh. "You don't mind, do ya?"

"No, that's okay," In reality, I thought baseball was one of the most boring things on the planet. Eddie loved it though, and so did Kay and Mateah. And since he'd be spending a lot more time with Hank than I ever would, I guess it didn't matter. Though it would be kind of annoying to have to tell Hank, and Clint, and Blake, and every other aloo we ended up getting, that no, I didn't watch the baseball game last night every single morning for all eternity.

"Why are you painting them?"

"These three guys here look the same as each other so I'm painting their name on their chests. That way you can tell who's who just by looking at them as easily as I can tell you're you."

"But they all have different coloured eyes, so you can already tell them apart. Hank's are yellow, and these guys have blue and green eyes. Which one of you is which, anyway?" I asked.

The robots and Eddie all stood motionless and silent.

"Uh, hello?"

"Auden, come on man, you gotta say their names. Watch this. Hey Clint!"

"YES, EDDIE?" the aloo on the right responded, his blue eyes flickering with each syllable he spoke.

"There ya go. Clint has blue eyes, Hank has yellow eyes, and Blake has green eyes. Think that's going to help you tell them apart when you're looking at 'em from behind or from across the job site, or should I just continue painting their names on them?" Eddie said, a puddle of sarcasm forming under the dripping brush in his hand.

"No, it's fine, it's a good idea. So when did Clint and Blake here show up?"

I was asking Eddie, but the aloos' eyes lit up at the sound of their names and responded in unison. "WE WERE FIRST ACTIVATED ON JANUARY

THIRTEENTH, 2053, DECLARED FIT FOR WORK ON JANUARY THIRTY FIRST, 2053, SHIPPED FROM THE ERIS INDUSTRIES FACTORY IN LOS ANGELES, CALIFORNIA, ON MARCH TWELFTH, 2053, TO THE WAREHOUSE IN MONTREAL, QUEBEC, WHERE WE ARRIVED ON MARCH TWENTY FIRST 2053, SOLD TO THE CONSTRUCTION FIRM EDCON ON APRIL TWENTY NINTH, 2053, SHIPPED TO TORONTO, ONTARIO, ON MAY FIRST, 2053, AND DEPLOYED TO THIS WORKSITE ON MAY SEVENTEENTH, 2053."

"Uh, thanks. That's today, right?"

"Yeah, they just got here this morning. Hank here is working out good so they sent us two more."

"Are Clint and Blake the same as Hank?"

"Exactly the same, yeah," Eddie started to say, but was interrupted by the robotic chorus.

"THE UNIT DESIGNATED HANK IS AN HNK SERIES EIGHT ZERO FIVE THREE MODEL, RUNNING AYY ELL YEW-OS NINE DECIMAL TWO THREE DECIMAL FIVE SEVEN. THE UNITS DESIGNATED CLINT AND BLAKE ARE HNK SERIES EIGHT ZERO FIVE THREE MODELS, RUNNING AYY ELL YEW-OS NINE DECIMAL TWO THREE DECIMAL FIVE NINE."

"Are they always going to do that?"

"Yeah, it's weird, isn't it? Anyway, I guess they're running a different OS version but Clint and Blake are the same as Hank."

This time Hank joined in, adding a third note to the chorus and rounding out a perfect minor chord.

"THE UNIT DESIGNATED HANK IS CREATED FROM PARTS BUILT IN SHENZHEN, CHINA. THE UNIT DESIGNATED CLINT IS CREATED FROM PARTS BUILT IN SHENZHEN, CHINA, AND TIANJIN, CHINA. THE UNIT DESIGNATED BLAKE IS—"

"Shut the fuck up, all of you! You're the same! God damn!" Eddie shouted, but the aloos continued.

"—BUILT IN TAIPEI, TAIWAN, AND—"

"Shut up, shut up, fuck's sake!"

"—ASSEMBLED IN THE ERIS INDUSTRIES INDUSTRIAL—"

"Why won't they shut up?"

"—LOS ANGELES, CALIFORNIA, AND—"

"Aren't you supposed to say their names?" I said.

"—SHIPPED TO THE WAREHOUSE IN—"

"Oh yeah," said Eddie. "Clint, Blake, Hank, shut the fuck up!"

"OKAY, EDDIE," said the chorus. "WE CAN SEE THAT YOU ARE UPSET, AND APOLOGIZE PROFUSELY FOR ANY ROLE WE MAY HAVE PLAYED IN THE DETERIORATION OF YOUR EMOTIONAL STATE."

"It's fine, just shut up," said Eddie.

"So uh, how are they doing?"

"Great, actually! I figured out you don't gotta tell them what to do piece by piece. You just gotta show them the schematic for the area you're working on and they do it all for you. Then you gotta take a look and make sure they didn't mess nothin' up, then you show them the next area and they do it again. I ain't gotta do nothin' now man, and I can still go home and feel like I put in a full day's work, it's great. Here, watch this. Hey Hank!"

"YES, EDDIE?"

"Look, this is what we're working on today," A blue-swathed projection arose from the phone in Eddie's hand. He had one of those cool new phones I was thinking about getting, the ones that looked a bit like a flatter hockey puck—it was even all black. It didn't have a screen, just the projection that floated a few inches above it. Seemed like kind of a bad idea, since you'd be broadcasting whatever you were watching to everyone around you. Maybe Eddie didn't care.

He brought up a projection of the building's schematic on his phone and pointed into the blue light. "Right here, picking up where we left off yesterday. You think you can show Clint and Blake what to do, Hank?"

"BECAUSE WE ARE CONNECTED TO EACH OTHER VIA THE ERISWEB 7G NETWORK, CLINT AND BLAKE ALREADY KNOW WHAT I KNOW," said Hank.

"WE ARE PREPARED TO EXECUTE THE TASK YOU REQUESTED," the three said together. "SHOULD WE BEGIN NOW?"

"Yep Hank, do it," said Eddie.

The three aloos made their way toward the building, the sound of a single footstep accompanying their strides.

A beam of light zigzagged across the work site as the aloos walked away—the sunshine traveling from the Sun to the wall of the mirrored glass condo building nearby to the aloos' reflective vest oscillated back and forth across my eyes like a pendulum, or a pulsar, or an aloo-operated lighthouse.

"Easy, huh?" said Eddie. "I wish they said what they had to say with not so many words. Actually, I was about to go grab some coffees. You want one?"

"No thanks, I should get up to the crane."

"Yeah, yeah, go ahead man."

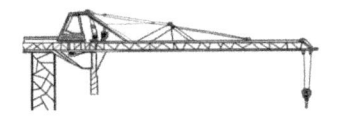

I'd like to say I was more prepared than the rest. That I had seen the warning signs and made the proper preparations. That I evacuated well before the government had given the official order. Truth is, I was skiing up in Aspen on what was supposed to have been a relaxing vacation before returning to my regular life. It was dumb luck that saved me, nothing more.

Still, I might have made it out anyway. Most of the people I know did.

It wasn't so bad, actually. At least as far as evacuations of major cities go.

But my home is still gone. Obliterated from the map.

And I don't mean that in the way someone from the Spanish Sahara might. Sure, their country no longer exists in a political sense, but the land is still there. They can stand in the place where their home once was, even if all that remains is a pile of rubble, or a country with a different name.

If you stand on the new West Coast of the United States, all you can see are a few buildings jutting out from above the ocean on the horizon. There's no actual ground to stand on. That's all that's left of my home.

That's all that's left of Los Angeles.

Some people still live in those buildings, too. There were so many unclaimed luxury yachts floating around after the flood and abandoned condos that the city's poor couldn't resist swiping them all up and living like royalty, setting up makeshift docks off a balcony or fire escape.

Can you imagine going from being crammed into a basement bachelor apartment with three other people, while doing your best to make it as an actor or a musician, to parading around in the living room of a multi-million dollar penthouse suite in a thousand dollar kimono and drinking a ten thousand dollar bottle of cognac out of a set of Grammys some rock star left behind?

And there were lots of Grammys to be found. Oscars too, and Tonys, and Emmys, and all the other showbiz awards you can think of. Naturally, most of the celebrities evacuated with the first warning, and most could think of more important things to grab than their accolades. The police and government officials evacuated too, as did most of the common folk. Those who stayed behind fit into three broad categories.

First, the intensely stubborn. These were people who lived in Los Angeles their entire lives and refused to evacuate their homes for anything. The public found them charming, cute, noble even, showing up on all sorts of news programs and reality shows. There's something about standing strong and proud in the face of unbelievable odds that just appeals to the average American. Everyone was rooting for them.

Most of them died, and quickly. A few still held out in their little corner of the world though. One of them even does a regular HoloTube show, vlogging about daily life in what's left of the city.

Next, the poor; those who weren't able to evacuate the city, even in the face of the apocalypse. These were single parents, immigrant workers, addicts, homeless teenagers, and a whole lot of people in already tough situations who found themselves in a tougher one. These people were exploited and marginalized before the flood, and not much has changed, though a few of them snatched up those luxury condos while they were still available.

Finally, the opportunistic. Mostly people with a criminal streak, these were the people who recognized the resources combined with the lawlessness and saw an opportunity to carve out their own little empire. Some of them had actually come to Los Angeles after the flood.

The buildings in which these little empires emerged were never designed to be submerged, though. Most structural engineers say they'll be rubble within a few years from the corrosive effects of the ocean water and the softening of the. Still, some of the groups are looking for ways to keep the buildings standing. To keep the city alive. I don't see the point of clinging to a carcass, but that's their prerogative.

But that doesn't mean I have no reason to return to Los Angeles.

The largest and most powerful group call themselves The Council. They've set up shop in The Hall, their new name for the old Los Angeles City Hall, and claim to be the legitimate government of the city, though nothing other than the building they live in gives them any real claim to that.

Through hydroponics and solar and hydroelectric power, they have the food and electricity they need to sustain themselves, and anything else they need they either trade for or (more often) take from the neighbouring communities by force.

The Hall is as heavily guarded as a pirate's treasury. I don't know how many snipers they have peering out the windows of that long, tall spire, but it's enough to shoot anyone they don't recognize on site. But like a pirate's treasury, there are enormous riches to be found there.

I used to be a city councillor for Los Angeles District 8 before all this. Maybe you recognize my name from those election signs, the ones in a shade of blue that my campaign team told me would demonstrate my liberal leanings without alienating too many conservative voters. Anyway, I know about the different parts of the building where the city kept its treasury, including one of the biggest vaults in one of The Hall's sub-basements. And as far as I know, The Council doesn't know about it.

If I'm right, and if I can get to the vault, and if I can access it, I'd be set for life. That's a lot of ifs, but it's worth a shot. And that's why I'm sitting in this hellhole of a casino a few blocks from the Nevada coastline in Primm. If I can find a captain to—

"Hey Auden! It's lunch time, pal," Sam's voice said over the cabin radio. "Why don't you come down and join us today?"

I liked to have lunch with the guys. It gave me a chance to shed my antisocial persona and spend some time with other people, which my therapist told me I should do more of (back when I bothered to see her; it had been years). But I also liked to have lunch in my cabin because it was more interesting. Besides, climbing up and down the crane once a day was enough. Today, the former impulse won, and after reaching the ground I found myself in the food trailer.

I grabbed a coffee from the food printer, unpacked my lunch, and sat down with the guys.

The aloos were still working tirelessly in the background, adding a level of slightly heightened tension to the atmosphere. It always felt a little wrong to take a break while others were working, and that seemed to hold true even if those other people aren't actually people.

I had begun to join the conversation in a way one does when they show up in the middle of things and have nothing to contribute other than by smiling and nodding as they figure out what's being talked about, which is to say I hadn't yet said a damn thing, when I heard a loud bang from behind me.

My heart was like an elevator torn free of its main cable. I turned around to see Eddie storming out of Byron's office trailer, having slammed the door off its hinges. His face couldn't have been sourer if he had just sucked the life out of a box of lemons.

"What the?" started Gael.

"Can you fucking believe it?" he shouted as he approached the table we sat at, gravel rattling at the back of his throat. "They replaced us with those fucking piece of shit robots. They shit-canned us, man! We're fucking fired! Fuck!"

"Come on Eddie yer overreacting, it ain't like that," Byron called after him but Eddie clearly wasn't listening.

"How the fuck could you fucking do this to me!?!" he roared at Byron, each word escorted by a barrage of spit, phlegm, and pointed fingers. "You promised me you wouldn't! You lying piece of shit! What the fuck am I going to do now huh!? What the fuck am I going to do!?" He stood staring at Byron, fists clenched, body trembling, betrayal leaking from his eyes.

"Eddie, c'mon man," said Avery, who along with Noble had emerged from Byron's office shortly after. He walked over to Eddie and put a hand on his shoulder. Eddie slapped it away without breaking eye contact with Byron. Grit his teeth hard enough that I could have sworn I saw a spark fly from his mouth.

After a moment, he stomped off, cursing and kicking anything in his path.

"I guess we should leave him be for now, huh?" said Leopold.

"Probably best. I'll talk to him later. Uh, go back to what you was doin' I guess," Byron said as he turned back into his office. Mateah disagreed, though, leaving her half-eaten sandwich behind to chase him.

"Why did he flip like that?" said Avery as he and Noble joined us. "We weren't fired, we were bottom lined. This is a good thing. We're free now."

"Yeah, I'm looking forward to it too," said Noble.

"All three of you were bottom lined today? Sam, did you know about this?" Karter asked.

In the distance, a faint expletive, a thump, and the clangs of a pile of material falling over, sandwiched by another expletive.

"Yeah, the order came from head office a few days ago. Byron and I have been talking about it since then, trying to figure out a way to break it to the crew tactfully. We thought we had it figured out, but I guess not."

"I mean whatever it is you think you figured out," said Gael, "do the opposite of that next time."

"What was that all about?" asked Gill as he sat down with us, a ketchup-drenched sandwich from the food printer in his hand.

"Eddie got bottom lined," said Avery. "So did Noble and I."

"No shit. I figured I'd be the first one to go," said Gill.

"Frankly Gill, you're the cheapest guy to pay per hour right now," said Sam. "Besides, Byron wanted to hold off for a few more weeks until you're finished your apprenticeship so you'll get a better bottom line cheque."

"Huh, that's weird," Gill breathed with a surprisingly pensive look. "I don't know, it's pretty great that I won't have to work anymore, but it almost seems like, I dunno, a letdown. I'm gonna go right from apprenticeship to retirement, you know? I mean, I'm not an old man. I got energy. I can work."

"I don't mind," said Noble. "I just finished my apprenticeship three years ago, and believe me it's not too exciting once you become a full carpenter."

"Yeah, and I finished mine just before Noble," said Avery. "Is that why we were bottom-lined first?"

"Yes exactly, you and Noble have the least seniority of all the carpenters at the full pay grade."

Avery shrugged matter-of-factly, timed just so to look like it triggered the latest crash. A shriek, a thump, and a bang punctuated it like an ellipsis.

"Okay, so why Eddie? He's been here longer than I have," said Kay. "Longer than most of us, actually."

"Eddie's strength is training the new guys," said Sam. "And since there aren't going to be any more new guys any time soon, it seemed to make sense."

"You know his attitude about the bottom line though. He's not exactly subtle about it. You had to know he was going to react like that," said Kay.

"Yeah, we did. But he was going to get bottom lined one way or another, so it was better to do it early. Either way he'd be angry about it, but at least this way it doesn't cause trouble on the job site and things stay on schedule."

"So what are you guys going to do now?" I asked.

"I don't know, I hadn't thought much about it," said Avery. "I guess I'll take some time to relax. Do some partying, have some fun, you know?"

"That's your life plan? To party?" asked Leopold.

"Why not? If I keep getting paid no matter what I do, why wouldn't I do what I enjoy most?"

"But isn't that going to get old after a while?"

"Maybe. If it does, I'll find something else to do. Why do I have to have my whole life figured out right now?"

"Good point. I guess I'll end up doing what I love too," said Noble.

"Which is?" asked Kay.

"I uh, I don't know yet. I guess I'll figure it out."

"I guess that's what we'll all have to do."

"Not Eddie, apparently" said Gill.

"Yeah, what do you think he's going to do now?" said Avery. "He's always complaining about the bottom line bums, but now he's one of them—err, one of us. That's gotta sting."

My mind ran through the catalogue of things one said about someone who'd just lost their job, picking out one that seemed the least ill-fitting for the situation. "Maybe he'll find a new place to work."

"Don't be ridiculous Auden. There are no new places to work," said Draven. "And even if he did find a new job, it's only a matter of time before another aloo comes along and replaces him there. We're all going to be replaced. They all want us to be good complacent little slaves and give us just enough to survive while they—."

"You're right, he's going to have to go on the bottom line," said Gael, cutting off Draven while he still made sense. "Unemployment was pretty high last I checked."

"Yeah, and the jobs that do pop up aren't in construction either," said Leopold. "I was helping my little cousin look through some of the job listings the other day, and there's not much out there. Social workers, cops, teachers, and the odd serving gig. That's about it. And I don't think Eddie's qualified for any of those."

"How does that work, anyway?" asked Kay. "Like, you get a bottom line cheque based on the amount of money you made while you were working, right? But what happens if you never had a job before?"

"I looked that up," said Leopold. "You're still supposed to get in touch with a company and apply for a job, then they immediately put you on the bottom line. That way, they still have backup workers in case something goes wrong."

"Yeah I remember that," said Gill. "I did a few interviews, but I went with you guys because you were the only company where I could actually fucking work instead of dicking around at home all day."

"What's wrong with you guys?" Avery asked. "Why would you want a new job anyway? It's not like you need one. You can do anything you want, you get all the money you need, and you choose to go get another job? Really, listen to yourselves for a minute. You can't think of a single thing you'd rather do than show up here every day and work as hard as we do every day, day in day out, for the next forty years?"

"Yeah, I like working here," said Noble, "but only because I need to work to get money. Now that I don't, I'll find something better to do with my time."

"I don't know, it seems like it would get old quickly," said Leopold. "I'm not going to react like Eddie, but he's not totally wrong. I'm not looking forward to it."

"I guess you could volunteer somewhere, maybe?" I, err, volunteered.

"I looked that up too," said Leopold, "when I was helping my cousin. Every charity we looked at didn't need any help, at least in terms of people. I guess people kind of all have the same ideas for what to do with themselves when they have nothing to do, huh?"

"You can't rely on anyone else. You have to find your own purpose," said Draven, for once offering a bit of actual insight.

"Yeah, I guess you could like, start your own charity or something?" said Brynlee.

"Sure," said Mateah, "but charities are there to solve a problem, so you'd have to figure out what problems there are that aren't already being addressed by another charity. And I don't know if you're creative enough for that one, Mr. Pac-Sterminator."

"I'm sure I could find something interesting to do with my time," said Kay.

"Yeah, I'm sure you could," said Gael with a sly smile, wagging his eyebrows like the needle on a polygraph test.

"Watch it," said Kay.

"Yeah, watch it," said Mateah, who socked Gael in the shoulder as she returned to her sandwich.

"Well?" asked Brynlee.

"He's not good," Mateah shook her head. "Wouldn't stop screaming and kicking things. I think I calmed him down enough that he's not going to do anything stupid." She pursed her lips, along with the rest of her face. "Of course, that was after he took a swing at me."

"He what?" asked Sam, pushing his chair back and jumping to his feet.

"Relax. I blocked it. I'm sure I'll have a nice bruise on my arm, but I'm fine. I don't know about Eddie, though. Once he did it, he muttered an apology and walked away."

"At least you wiped that sour look off his face," said Avery.

"Yeah, I've never seen anyone so pissed in my life," said Gael.

Neither had I. He was like a cornered animal. At least, I think he was. I've never actually seen a cornered animal, other than a squirrel or something, but they can escape pretty easily so I don't think that counts. There's that old saying about cornered animals that people always bring up whenever they talk about a person acting viciously, and I don't think they're talking about squirrels, but probably something more, like a dog or a tiger or a cheetah.

And I think that's what I mean too.

But other than Draven, no one seemed interested in acknowledging the question that must have been on everyone's minds: When would I be replaced? When would I be joining the legions of redundant workers?

And not only that, what would I do once I was among them? For the first time in as long as I could remember, I had no idea what my future was going to look like, and I didn't even know where to start trying to figure it out.

"HELLO AUDEN. DID YOU WATCH THE BLUE JAYS GAME LAST NIGHT?" I heard a robotic voice ask me as I walked by toward the crane. It might have been Hank, or Clint, or Blake, or maybe we got a new one. I didn't bother looking.

# 9

Later that evening, we all went out for a celebratory drink at The Black Cat. Everyone was there except Byron and Sam, who don't usually join us anyway. I think Byron was thinking about breaking that tradition considering the unique circumstances. Eddie's response earlier seemed to make it clear Byron was the last person he'd want to see, other than maybe whomever it was that sold us those aloos in the first place.

I don't know what he did for the rest of the day, but whatever it was, it didn't dull his anger. His body was still as tense as before, his face twisted and crumpled like the fender of a crashed car. He took any opportunity he could to kick whatever he found in his way—including the door, for which Arya gave him an earful. At least he wasn't yelling anymore.

The rest of the crew gave him a wide berth—especially Mateah, who'd developed a purple welt on her forearm. They headed over to the left side of the bar, while Eddie walked over to the empty seat on the right, plopped himself down on it, ordered a whisky, and sulked. A bunch of barflies separated him from the rest of the crew, and nobody really seemed to mind the arrangement.

I didn't want to sit with him, but apparently neither did anyone else, and you can't leave someone alone when they're obviously so upset. Besides, I'm used to being separated from the rest of the crew.

As he drank, he fingered the charm on his necklace. It was a cheap little pewter thing, three circles in the shape of a pyramid hanging from a piece of brown jute cord. Eddie once said it was a rare and valuable charm his parents had brought back from their travels when they were young, and it brought him good luck.

I recognized it as the logo from one of those music festivals that were popular in the early 21st century when our parents were young and hedonistic—my mom had one, and tens of thousands of others must have as well, but I didn't have the heart to tell him that. Especially not right now.

"Guess my luck ran out," he muttered to himself. He raised his empty glass and waggled it at Arya, the bartender. "Another one of these."

"Sure thing, Eddie," Arya poured another drink and slid it across the bar to Eddie. "I've never seen you so bummed out before. What's up?"

"I got bottom lined, Arya. I can't believe it."

"That's good though, isn't it?" Arya asked, tucking her colourful hair behind her ear. It fell out almost immediately. "Doesn't that mean you don't have to work anymore?"

"Yeah."

"And you get free money from the government, right?"

"Yeah." He didn't so much say the *yeah*s as he exhaled them.

"I don't get it. That sounds great to me. What's there to be sad about?"

"Yeah, look on the bright side, Eddie." I clapped him on the shoulder to punctuate the following statement with far more confidence than I felt. "Now you don't have to work anymore. You're free, man."

"But what am I supposed to do?"

"Whatever you want," said Arya. "If I had all that free time, I'd be so happy! I'd finally be able to do what I've always wanted to do and write a book. I've always had this idea for a book but I've never had time to write it. It's about this family, the Pikes. They're a real wholesome family, a husband and wife with twin sons and a daughter. They go on a road trip and stay the night in a bed and breakfast in the countryside in West Virginia where they meet another family, the Autumns, and become friends.

"The Autumns invite the Pikes to their home for dinner one evening because they don't live too far away, and at dinner the Pikes find out the Autumns are a bunch of ultra-religious loonies who believe God told them to purify the world of sinners. They lock the main character, the youngest Pike daughter, in the basement away from the rest of the family because they decided she's the biggest sinner of the group because she was wearing a black shirt with a skull on it. She ends up escaping and helps the rest of her family escape, but not before killing each of the Autumns one by one—each death more gruesome than the last. The last Autumn she kills is the father, and he beats the hell out of the Pike daughter before she grabs an axe and buries it in his forehead. Then they light the Autumns' house on fire and drive away. The parents are relieved that they escaped from the evil Autumns, but after seeing what their daughter did to escape, they can't help but think they're taking the greatest evil with them."

"That's really dark, Arya."

"Yeah, I love horror. I know it doesn't make any sense, but it keeps me positive. Anyway, I have the whole story mapped out in my head, and I even have part of it written out in a few notebooks at home. But I don't know if I'll ever have time to write it with everything I have to do to run this place."

"What if you bought an aloo?" I asked. "If you own the place, can't you just, like, bottom line yourself?"

"Ugh, bartender aloos are the worst. There's a bar in the condo building across the street with a bartender aloo and nobody goes there because it's like ordering a drink from a vending machine. Would you boys keep coming by if you got your drinks from a robot?"

"Yeah that's great for you, but what if I want to work?" said Eddie, clearly not interested in anyone else's problems.

"What if you worked for Arya?" I asked. "Like, help her bartend or something?"

"I'd love that," said Arya, having ever-so-briefly shot me a look that told me I'd way overstepped my bounds, "but right now I'm happy doing things on my own. I don't really need any help. You'll find something to do, though, I know it."

Eddie sighed and rolled his eyes, tired of the pointless platitudes we were giving him.

"Keep smiling Eddie, you'll be okay," said Arya, pouring out three shots of vodka. "Here, on me. And one for you too, Auden. To endless possibilities," she held the glass up. As the vodka snaked down my throat, my face mirrored Eddie's and I was reminded why I prefer wine.

"Just keep coming to see me here, Eddie. That's one thing you can do, at least," Arya moved on to the next customer. "I'll find some way to cheer you up."

"She doesn't get it." Eddie stared into his glass. "No one does. What am I supposed to do now?"

"You can always try finding another job."

He let out a long sigh, emptied his glass, and ordered another. "That's what Arya just said man, come on. Pay attention. There aren't any other jobs out there. Not for a guy like me."

Arya slid him another drink and smiled a smile that was equal parts sympathetic and confused.

"What about baseball?" I asked.

"What *about* baseball?"

"You like baseball, right? Why don't you do that?"

"The hell are you talking about, 'do baseball?' How am I going to 'do baseball?'"

"I don't know, like, join a team or something, or write a book about baseball, I don't know."

"I'm 46 years old, Auden. I got cricks in my knees, my back's always sore, and my shoulder's still messed up from the Davenport job a few years back. Nobody's going to want me to play baseball with 'em. And I ain't no good with words neither."

I ran out of ideas, and decided silence was preferable to conversation at that point. Eddie fixed his gaze directly ahead at nothing in particular, his entire body a statue, other than the one arm occasionally raising his glass to his lips and the other flagging down Arya for more liquor.

Around us, the rest of the crew were feeding Avery and Noble drink after drink of who-knows-what. The two of them had laid their heads back on the bar while Arya poured vodka into each of their mouths, while the rest of the group cheered.

The gravity of their mirth attracted several others, including a few women from the dance floor with whom Gael and Avery had flapped and gyrated moments before. Gael's latest conversation ended with a slap in the face. I didn't hear what he said but he probably deserved it—this wasn't the first time I'd seen that happen. He shrugged it off and bought everyone another round of drinks. If they noticed Eddie and me at all, they didn't show it.

I leaned over on the bar, wrapping my thumb around the edge of it and feeling the old beads of dried wood stain clinging to it, drips frozen in time. Three of them hung down side by side like tiny stalactites at the mouth of a cave inside which you might find untold riches or a wild animal waiting to devour you and feed you to its young. I read these three bumps like Braille before picking away at them like a neurotic excoriator. Two came away easily, but the last one hung firmly in place, unwilling to be evicted from the place it had called home for the last few dozen years.

"What about travelling?" Arya brought over our share of the shots Gael bought everyone. "Have you ever travelled? They have those LifeSim things now where you can travel wherever you want without leaving your house. A friend of mine has one. She and I went to Ibiza last weekend and it was amazing. It really felt like we were there. You should try it too. I'm thinking of getting one for the bar that people can rent, you know, by the hour sort of thing."

"Nah..."

"Well do you know anything about fixing electronics? Maybe I could hire you to maintain it for me."

"I dunno nothin' about no 'lectronics," Each word dripped out of Eddie's mouth.

Arya shrugged. "Okay, well, let me know when you're ready for another drink."

"Jus' keep 'em coming," he echoed into his empty glass.

The final drop was still stuck to the bar edge. I dug at it from multiple angles, using multiple digits, at one point bending the nail on my middle finger backward and folding it over itself. I put my weight behind the push, my body twitching forward each time my finger slipped. I'm sure the people around me assumed I'd had a few too many, and they might have been right.

The harder I pushed, the more it resisted.

Another shot arrived—if I drank it, I didn't notice. It was more than a drip now; it was the focus of my being. The entirety of my life until now had prepared me for this moment. Nothing existed except for my fingers and this drip. The reason was no longer relevant. It had to find a weakness I could exploit, some angle I could claw through to tear it out. Finally, it snapped free, silently joining its companions in a pile of dust on the ground.

"Hey, c'mon, chin up man," Avery staggered over and flopped his arm like a dead carp over Eddie's shoulder. "Now you can do whatever you want."

"Fuck off, Avery," Eddie shoved the other man's arm away. "And fuck all of you!"

He slapped his phone on the payment receiver on the bar and stormed out, jacket in hand.

*Oh yeah,* I thought, *I was going to ask Eddie about his phone.*

Avery shrugged and walked back over to where the other guys were chatting.

What I thought I could accomplish by my next action, I still have no idea. It seemed like the right thing to do though; you can't let your friend storm out of the bar that upset without making sure they're okay, right? I probably wasn't the most qualified person on Earth for the job, but obviously neither were Arya or Avery.

If they were interviewing candidates for the position and the three of us showed up, they would have chosen me only because my general lack of experience altogether looked good when compared with their experience in utterly failing at the job. I was far from the best, but perhaps the least worst.

I followed Eddie out of the bar and into the blue haze of the street lights outside. It took my eyes a moment to adjust.

"Eddie, hold on," I called to a figure I was pretty sure was him.

"Get lost!" Eddie's voice snapped from behind me.

"Come on man, why do you have to be like that?" I asked after catching up with him. "I just wanted to ask you about your phone."

"What? Yours dead or something?"

"No, I was curious about it. It looks cool. Is it a good phone?"

"What are you on about now? My entire life has fallen apart and you're asking for phone advice? You're a weird guy."

"I'm trying to help. It's not that bad."

"Not that bad?" He turned around and looked straight into my eyes as he pulled his jacket on. Never had the two inches of height Eddie had over me seemed so significant. I did my best to meet his gaze.

"What do you know about 'not that bad'? And don't give me that 'you can do whatever you want' bullshit either. Everyone in my family does 'whatever they want.' None of them have ever even had a job man, you know how pathetic that is? My brother has five kids from five different mothers, my cousin never leaves her house, and my nephews are all junkies. Bunch of losers, all of them. Even my parents were losers too.

Pissed their lives away partying like a bunch of mindless morons.

"I'm the only one in my family who's got a job man. I ain't no doctor or a lawyer or nothin', but what I got I worked for. I never asked for no handout. What am I going to do now, be another waste of space? Drift through life like the rest of my useless family? You don't know nothing man, so fuck off."

All I could think of was what all those government ads said about the bottom line. "It's not a handout though man. It's like graduating to a new stage in your life. You put in your time and now you get to move on and—" *don't say do whatever you want...* "—and make your life into something different."

"I've heard that before man, that's what everyone says," he shouted. "It's like graduating, it's like freedom, do whatever you want, to hell with all that. That's not what I want." I opened my mouth to reply, but he cut me off. "And then you tell me to find another job. You know, you're clueless man. You spend so much time up in that crane that you don't know nothing about the world around you. There ain't no more jobs out there. Everyone's getting replaced. They're going to replace you soon too. You ever think about what you're going to do with your life when they take away your purpose?"

"I don't know yet, but there's gotta be something."

"So that's your big plan? You spend all day by yourself up in that crane and you haven't even thought of what you're going to do? No wonder you're just saying what everyone else says, like a parrot. They're coming for your purpose, you better figure it out pal."

"What else can I do? I haven't figured it out yet. You'll figure it out too. There's something for you."

"There's nothing for me. I got replaced before by those goddamn 3D house printers ten years ago. They can finish a whole house in a couple of hours man. Plumbing, heating, electricity, insulation, everything. All it takes is one asshole with one working thumb to push a button and bam, new house. There ain't no more jobs there. And now I'm pushed out of the high-rise thing too. There's robots to build new houses, robots to fix old houses, robots to pave the streets, robots to build cabinets, robot welders, robot iron workers, robot boilermakers, robot landscapers, robot fucking everything, man. And I ain't got no book smarts, man; the only thing I ever did was work with my hands, and nobody needs no one who works with their hands. What else can I do?"

He took a deep breath and lowered his voice. "This is the last time I'll join you guys as equals. This is the last day I'll earn my pay for a hard day's work."

I pursed my lips. What could I say to that? What would you have said?

"Look, work is all I got man," Eddie paced back and forth on the sidewalk. "I gave my life to it. I got no kids and I never got married. I got my girl Kyrie yeah, but we ain't never going to be serious. I treat her like shit and she gives it right back to me. So what do I got? I got my shitty apartment, I got my shitty girlfriend who ain't even talking to me right now, and I got my job. Except now I ain't even got that. I ain't got nothin' now, man. I got nothing going for me no more. There's no point. It's hopeless man, you don't know."

Up until that point I was keeping as tight-lipped as I could despite the insults he was hurling at me. Since I spent most of my time up in the crane anyway, it's not like the outcome of an argument ever mattered much. But the pressure of Eddie's attitude built up in me like champagne behind a cork, my annoyance at the fact that I had been stuck listening to the guy whine all night while the rest of the crew enjoyed themselves had untwisted the muselet, and the latest string of insults he laid on me had popped the cork.

"You're being an idiot, Eddie. My dad would have killed to have the bottom line. He lost job after job when I was a kid and then he died."

"I don't give a—" Eddie began to interrupt.

"No, shut up and let me finish, for once in your goddamn life. My dad died when I was sixteen because he didn't have the bottom line. He couldn't feed his family or put a roof over their heads and the stress of it killed him. It killed him. He's dead. That's what real hardship is like. You're taken care of, man; you can find something to fill your time with. You've been given a free ride for the rest of your life and you're acting like someone told you you've got six months to live. Quit pouting like a baby and grow up."

My anger fizzled like a science fair volcano after spending all its vinegar. Eddie's motionless face came back into focus, his eyebrows raised higher than a clown's. I glared at him, as surprised by the outburst of frustration I didn't even know I had in me as he was. We stood in confused silence for a moment before I recovered my usual composure.

My boots were clean.

"Go back to the bar, Auden." Eddie said after what felt like a thousand moments. "I'll see you around. It's been, uh, nice working with you, man. Sorry I yelled at you. Take care."

He turned around and walked away. What was I supposed to do? Chase him again? Try to talk some sense into him? Grab him by the shirt collar and drag him back to the bar? Run up behind him and punch him in the back of the head? My newfound courage and boldness planted all these ideas in my mind. While I contemplated which action to take, Eddie's silhouette grew smaller.

He kicked a garbage can over, spewing its contents across the sidewalk. He crossed the street in front of traffic, to the sound of angry horns and blaring expletives. He threw the door of the maglev station open, skipping the automatic doors.

I stared for a few moments at the point where his silhouette disappeared, noticing the building and the people walking out of it. Somehow it managed to both blend in with the background of its surroundings and stand out at the same time.

The early 21st century design still seemed somehow at home amid the new condo buildings, as timeless as a leather jacket on top of a white t-shirt. If I didn't know what a maglev was, I'd be confused about how many people were coming out of the building. Then again, if I didn't know what a maglev was, I'd be pretty confused about a lot of things. Like why this metal underground serpent seemed to devour people whole and spit them out at random through the dozen mouths it had on the side of its body, and why people seemed to submit themselves willingly to it.

"What are you looking at?" I heard a voice behind me ask. I turned back around and saw Leopold standing outside the bar lighting one of those pastel green cigarettes he insisted on importing from England.

"Oh, Eddie left."

"Yeah I noticed you two weren't in there anymore. I went to the washroom, and when I came back you were both gone. Anyway, I'm not surprised. He's never seemed too thrilled about being bottom lined. I'm not too worried yet though, since the aloos can't weld so I should be safe for now. Anyway, how about you?"

At this point I realized Leopold must have come outside as I had turned around, otherwise he'd have known the answer to his question.

"I don't know yet," I peered in through the window around the Black Cat logo emblazoned on it. It was like the end of a film, most of the entire cast celebrating. Avery and Noble took a round of shots with the rest of the crew, except for Brynlee who was hunched over the Pac-Man machine. Draven, who sat by the side, shook his head. I could almost forget what happened. Almost.

I considered going back in, but the earful I'd gotten from Eddie hadn't exactly put me in a celebratory mood. And while Draven was the perennial party pooper, the definition of a buzz kill, that role was unfamiliar to me, and I'd had enough unfamiliarity for one night. I could always have a chat with him and learn about the reason the US invaded Morocco last year, but what was the point?

Besides, I already knew why the US had invaded Morocco: the Moroccan government discovered a portal to hell while finishing excavations of the ruins of an old Roman city and they were about to open it, unleashing all sorts of demons and devils and other icky horrors upon this plane of existence.

Draven had told us all about it last week. Look it up.

"You alright?" Leopold asked me.

"Yeah, why?"

"Your hands are shaking."

"I'm cold is all."

"How are you cold in this weather?"

"I uh, have a circulatory problem."

Leopold looked at me incredulously. "You're sure you're alright?"

"Yeah, yeah I'm fine. I'm going to head home. See you tomorrow?"

"Yeah, see you." I left, feeling a little guilty about not paying my tab, but Arya would understand, I'd hoped. I'd settle up next time.

Stupid as Eddie was acting, though, he had given me a lot to think about. What was I going to do after I was bottom lined? Was I looking forward to it?

Eddie wasn't because he'd never had a family of his own, I guess. I never married or had any kids either, but most people didn't these days. Sam had his family, and I think Byron was married too. Leopold had once talked about adopting a kid with his husband, but I don't think that ever panned out. Gael, Avery, Karter, and Noble were all single, and Gill probably was too. And Draven? Who knows.

I did have a woman I saw occasionally, Marlow. Maybe I should send her a message. She traveled a lot for her job as a salesperson for a software company, so between that and my job in the crane there wasn't much time for a committed relationship. I liked that fine, and so did she.

I sent her a message.

# 10

As I languished in Libby Prison, having been captured by the army of the Confederacy after suffering defeat at the battle of Charleston, the longing for liberty grew stronger day by day within the hearts of my fellow prisoners. Near me lay Lieutenant Moore and Captain Diaz, both clad in the same Union infantry uniform I donned, though the badge emblazoned on each of their shoulders marked them as members of the 38th Wisconsin regiment, whereas I belonged to the 13th Maryland. Based on our proximity to each other within our cell, they confided in me their plan of escape.

In the rear of the fireplace, Moore had discovered the mortar holding together the bricks to be quite loose and easy to chip away. The three of us took shifts in the evening, with one digging a tunnel behind the bricks, another fanning fresh air down the shaft with his hat, and the third standing guard against random inspection. This effort resulted in considerable hardship for our fellow prisoners, deprived of their only heat source..

While in the tunnel, the hearts within us trembled in fear of a cave in. Should a collapse occur, the concept of our surviving the crushing weight of the earth above us long enough for our fellow prisoners to dig us out was an impossible one.

Their only balm for this horror, and the only reason we collectively suffered this torment, was the prospect of a means of escape. We continued for several weeks as one of us in turn would use a spoon, a fork, or a stick from the fire, now pushing it forward, now pulling it back, loosening the Earth, each moment bringing us one step closer to freedom. Once we felt the tunnel of sufficient length to extend out of the prison walls, we resolved to begin preparations to break the surface and allow the escape to begin.

The evening before our escape, we made the full weight of our plans known to the rest of the prison populace. Liberty soon overcame all objections, save for three men, who opted to remain behind out of fear of reprisal, though they swore a solemn oath to refrain from revealing the details of our plot.

Organizing into groups of two, we agreed to stay by each other's side, ensuring liberty for both or for neither. Thirty eight men escaped from Libby Prison this way.

At about 9 o'clock at night, I passed through the tunnel with Lieutenant Moore as my companion. The tunnel emerged into a dimly lit yard nearby, and the two of us, having procured for ourselves civilian clothes from a nearby clothesline, proceeded to stroll along the street with the intention of appearing as casual as possible while maintaining haste.

We had not proceeded far when we were ordered by a single sentinel, in front of what appeared to be a hospital, to halt, which we did, in both our hearts and our feet. In response to his declaration of "Who goes there?" we responded, "We are citizens going home," in the best approximation of the Virginian vernacular, to which he replied, "You must know that no one is permitted to walk on this here sidewalk in front of this here hospital after dark! Take the side street." We politely acquiesced to his demands.

We were soon outside the city, and choosing for our guide the North Star, we pursued our journey. I heard a distant voice in the forest calling to me by name. Unsure of who would know me in this place, I and Lieutenant Moore passed quickly through a thicket of branches, now pushing them forward, now pulling them back, and into an old fallen treetop, falling flat on the ground and awaiting developments. A short time elapsed and we saw a figure stealthily approaching.

The lieutenant whispered "There is only one of them, and unless he is armed we can and will dispatch him."

The man came nearer and, once again calling me by name, I recognized him as Major Samuel Soyinka of the 24th Connecticut Infantry, our fellow prisoner at Libby. We arose from the ground, and he quickly recognized us.

"Auden Black, are you awake?" he called to me.

"Yes major, we are here. In our weary travels the lieutenant and I are grateful to see a familiar face."

"Auden, what the hell are you talking about? Snap out of it man."

"Oh, uh, hey Sam. What's up?"

"Aye aye, captain!" he responded. I could hear him making a mock salute.

"Sorry about that, heh."

"You're a weird guy Auden. What were you just doing?"

"I don't know," I muttered. "Anyway, you're probably busy so, uh, what's up?"

"Not really. Those aloos are getting so far ahead of the rest of us that I've been spending a lot of time sitting around waiting. I'm starting to feel like Eddie these days."

*Good, yes, let's talk about you instead, or Eddie, or anything other than me and what I was doing.*

"Is that so?"

"Yeah, things sure are different than they used to be. I'm having trouble getting used to it, and some of the other guys said the same. Not that it matters much anyway. Looks like we're all on the road to being replaced. Anyway, how did things go at the bar last night?"

"Avery and Noble seemed to have a good time. Eddie, not so much."

"I heard. Mateah told me Eddie spent the entire night fuming at the bar and then stormed out of the place."

"He was being ridiculous. We tried to cheer him up but he wasn't having it."

"I'm not surprised. He's taking this pretty hard."

"Yeah he said he was bottom lined once before," I said.

"He was. His old boss worked with Byron on a few projects, so when they had to let Eddie and the rest of the crew go he called Byron to see if he needed anyone. Poor guy was drinking like a fish and not doing much else."

"But he never wanted to work. He was such a slacker."

"Yeah he was, but for Byron it was more about helping someone out than getting a hard worker. And so long as Byron keeps things on budget and on schedule, head office doesn't ask too many questions." He paused a moment. "I probably shouldn't have told you that, but I know you'll keep it to yourself."

He was right, of course. Who else do I even talk to, anyway?

"Anyway, it's not like Eddie was useless. He did a good job of training the new guys. Ask Noble. He had nothing but good things to say when he was apprenticing under Eddie."

"Yeah."

I heard a voice in the background of the radio.

"Yeah, sure. Just a moment. Gotta run Auden, Brynlee needs a hand with something. Talk to ya later. Oh, and they're ready for another load of I-beams."

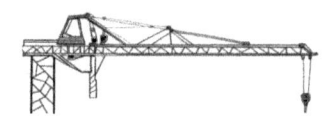

Major Soyinka, having joined our party, explained to us the fate of his companion, Major Stokowski. Having reached a fork in their path, the two majors disagreed on the next path to take. Major Soyinka insisted the left-hand would bring them northward, while Major Stokowski insisted the right-hand was the most expedient. Not being able to come to an agreement, the two majors decided to go their separate ways.

Our Major expressed a modicum of guilt over this, believing himself to have betrayed his compatriot, to which we replied that Major Stokowski and himself both sought liberty within their hearts, and each man must take his own path thereon towards.

This idea seemed to calm Major Soyinka somewhat, though he still showed concern for his companion.

Proceeding on foot from our meeting spot, we found a ravine through which ran a small stream of water, where we halted a few moments to rest. We soon began to climb a steep hill in our front. The ground was slippery, Virginia having been experiencing its rainy season, and as a result I found myself in the creek at the bottom of the hill. Emptying the water from my boots as best I could, I returned to the hill with surer footing and arrived at the summit.

Looking up, we spotted a rebel military base in front of us. We could not retrace our steps, and to do so would surely arouse the suspicions of the soldiers within the base, who by now had certainly noticed the three travellers before them.

The sentinel's announcement suggested our former masters in the prison were not yet alerted to our escape, or, if they were, the news had not yet traveled to this outpost. We concluded to pass directly through the camp. No one spoke to us, assuming us to be civilian travellers, and we did nothing to encourage conversation.

"Post number eight, ten o'clock and all is well," we heard a sentinel cry out. Our Major was heartened by the sentinel's announcement, taking it as news that his former companion remained free. Though he was our enemy, the three of us agreed with this sentinel wholeheartedly.

Proceeding onward, we deigned to remain within forests and wooded areas, avoiding roads altogether. This extended our journey, perhaps unnecessarily, but the possibility of the rebels being alerted to our escape became more and more certain with each step we took. The fewer people we encountered, the safer we would be.

We rested during the day, traveling only at night so as to further conceal our movements. We dared not build a fire, cold though the spring air was, so great was our desire to remain concealed.

Having crossed a set of railroad tracks I believed to be near Richmond, we walked through a thicket of forest before exiting to find another Confederate sentinel. Doubtlessly present only to alert the city of Union activity. Terror welled within our hearts and we fled to the relative security of the forest at the top of our speed, expecting to hear the crack of a rifle or a command to halt.

Upon finding an effective place to conceal ourselves, we realized the gentleman was asleep at his post. Nevertheless, we decided to rest a while, listening carefully for any notes we could bring back to the Star-Spangled Banner which may aid our cause.

As soon as darkness returned, we moved forward, weary, exhausted, and sore. Few words passed between us, with the exception of Major Soyinka's comment that he would be leaving our party.

"Auden, we're all done down here," he claimed. "Everyone's going home for the day."

"I do not understand, sir," I replied.

"Is the radio broken? Can you hear me? Auden, hello?"

Oh.

"Yeah, I can hear you now. What's up?"

"You are!" he said with a chuckle. "Everyone's heading home for the day, pal. Good work today. See you tomorrow."

"Yeah, see you Sam."

# 11

Nothing was on.

I mean, everything was on. Everything is still on. Everything is always on if you've got a HoloTube.

It gives you access to just about every show ever, even the older ones that don't use the full 360-degree range of vision the holoprojector creates. Feel like a sitcom? Select the option and you'll get a list of tens of thousands of shows, from *I Love Lucy* to *The Simpsons* to *Nevaeh's Big Score*.

How about a horror flick?

Go ahead and entertain yourself with the most terrifying rubber masks and marionette UFOs the 1950's could deliver, the tacky computer-generated creatures of the early 2000's, or the modern stuff so immersive that several people a year are found dead in their homes of heart attacks with some gore fest like *The Bludgeoning III* or *Room 666 at the Hotel Hell* at the top of their "recent views" list.

Serials, dramas, documentaries, comedies, romance, sci-fi, fantasy, kid's stuff, you name it. Dozens of new shows from each genre end up in the HoloTube's library every day in every language you can imagine. There are shows in dead languages like Latin or Esperanto, and even a morning talk show in Klingon. Pick your poison and you'll live a dozen lifetimes before you get to see even a fraction of what's out there.

But nothing was on. Nothing was ever on.

I considered resuming a documentary series I'd been watching on the American

Civil War or popping on a nature show, but after a few minutes of browsing the options, my mind ached for something else to do. Restless, I poked around my condo, tidying things up and keeping busy.

On the nights I didn't spend with Marlow (which was most of them) I ended up here wondering what to do with myself. What I ended up doing generally became one of the following:

I had already decided I didn't feel like watching the HoloTube. It wasn't the lack of choice offered on the HoloTube as much as the fact I was too antsy to enjoy sitting around. So that crossed reading and video games off the list too.

I always tried to avoid projecting at home unless I was incredibly bored. It was a fun way to pass the time at work, but if that's all I did, I'd probably have lost my mind altogether. The one exception was if I was at a great point in a story and wanted to see what happened next, which is kind of where I was with the Libby Prison projection.

But I'd finished up a projection at home yesterday on the Battle of Gettysburg, and I didn't want to do that twice in a row. So strike projecting off the list too.

I don't know why I kept that guitar. I hadn't played much more than a song or two since crane operating school, and even then I was never very good. And now I'm a fraction as good as I used to be. "Playing my guitar" shouldn't even really be considered as part of that list as much as "thinking about playing my guitar" should.

Speaking of school, I could always send one of my old pals from undergrad a message. But I hadn't kept up with them, and it felt weird to reach out after years had passed.

In retrospect, that's what I'd felt ever since I dropped out of university; I figured it was too soon to reach out right after because I didn't want to come across as desperate for friends or company or anything, so I figured I'd wait a few months to seem cooler, more likeable.

But by the time a few months had passed, I felt like everyone would have moved on with their lives and made new friends and probably graduated and gotten jobs and maybe gotten married and had kids and bought houses and all that other stuff and basically made a life that didn't involve me so why would they even care if I messaged them?

It had only been a few months at that point, so they wouldn't have graduated yet. I had overanalyzed the entire thing and let my imagination run wild, as usual. So if I had messaged them a few months after I dropped out, or even kept in touch right away, everything would have been fine. I'd still have a good group of friends. But now, with school having ended fifteen years ago, it seemed way too long.

Then again, maybe I'd look at this moment a few years from now and figure hey, fifteen years wasn't such a long time, I should have messaged them, but now it's been 20 years which is way too long.

I didn't message them.

The only real reason I ever had to clean my condo was when Marlow came over, and the last couple times I'd seen her at her place. It had gotten so bad that the act of picking up the broom would have created more of a mess from disturbing all the dust the broom itself had accumulated.

The takeout containers sitting on the counter were in various states of decomposition—they'd been getting pretty good at making these containers biodegrade quickly, to the point where they were completely gone within a month.

I never had more than a month's worth of takeout containers sitting on my counter. The ones there sat atop a patina of decomposed matter which grew higher and higher the longer I waited between cleaning, which I viewed through a haze of particles hanging in the air of my apartment because the fan that used to keep the air clear had broken and I hadn't put in a service order to call an aloo repair crew.

I rarely bothered to throw away the ones that were sitting there, since I figured things would take care of themselves, which they pretty much did.

Or at least that's what I told myself.

I could clean it. I should clean it. I should at least open the window. Or I should hire one of those aloo cleaning services. They send a robot to your house and it cleans each room in about ten minutes, with an extra minute allotted for washrooms.

They could clean my little bachelor condo in about half an hour. It's pretty amazing to watch, actually. You order the cleaner, and within a few minutes a plastic bin big enough to sit in shows up at your door or on your balcony (which I don't have), delivered by a drone. Inside the bin is the aloo, which makes its own way out and starts tackling your house. It's about the size and shape of a Frisbee, but it's flexible and wraps around whatever surface it crawls across, tailoring its cleaning attack to make sure it gets into the crevasses of your couch and the grout in your tiles and the gaps between the books on your shelf.

It goes back and forth over your house like the ink jets of a paper printer, and if you're like me and don't clean your house often you can actually see a visible line marking where the aloo has been and where the filth still lies.

Crawls up the walls and across the ceiling too. It seems like it would fall off, but it doesn't, and I haven't been able to figure out how it works.

Anyway, it grinds up everything it can and drops its waste in the plastic bin to be taken to a depot and separated into its constituent elements so it can be recycled, incinerated, or thrown in the trash as necessary.

I could call one and it would be here in a few minutes.

Maybe later.

Since going to Layla's Rumour meant a walk, the two options were one and the same. And since those were the only options left on my list, I grabbed my jacket and walked out the door.

Layla's Rumours was right smack in the corner of The Six Point Plaza, an L-shaped strip mall around the corner from my place near Bloor and Kipling. It was a bizarre sight to see when surrounded by condo buildings, but I guess whoever owns it hasn't wanted to sell it to the legions of developers who have doubtlessly been courting them.

Maybe they're holding out for a better deal.

Seemed to work well for the businesses in there. Most of the many condo buildings that have been built in the area have businesses set up in the ground floor, but they're mostly either doctor's offices or aloo operated convenience stores and coffee shops so artificial and boring that people usually only go there when they're in a rush.

Six Points, on the other hand, had more of a sense of permanence to it, a retro charm that had come in and out of fashion several times since it was built, probably back in the 1970's or something. These days, it's back in vogue, probably because it's so rare a sight to come across.

Along with Layla's Rumour there were a few other relics from the past. The Beanyards was a coffee shop famous these days for being staffed by actual humans instead of aloo-brews like every other shop around. Next door to The Beanyards was an actual bookstore staffed by actual people who love to read and who suggest books to you based on their experience rather than the suggestive algorithms you get online (which, to be fair, are actually quite good).

There was also a tailor, a sporting goods store, an accountant's office, a pizza place, and a pharmacy, each of which, paradoxically, staffed actual humans and were thriving businesses despite the fact that you could get anything they provided taken care of online within minutes of ordering it, and without so much as putting on a pair of pants.

This killed most other businesses, but somehow the business owners in Six Points Plaza were safe from it all. Stepping onto its property was like walking through a time machine. No, it was more like walking into an interactive museum exhibit. Take the audio tour, and let the British lady's soothing voice narrate your experience in cultural tourism from a couple dozen years ago.

Not that it was entirely a relic, mind you. There was a bank, a butcher shop, a dollar store, and a hair salon in the plaza too, all of which were aloo operated. But if you ignored them, and only went to the human operated stores, you could almost imagine what life was like back before aloos started showing up and the bottom line was a thing.

The walk to Layla's Rumour was one I'd made many times before, and as usual, I heard the place before I saw it. I guess a couple of years ago, the owner said something to upset a lot of people. I don't know what he said, but I know it was enough that a group of protesters had made it their mission to picket the place and generally make things difficult for owners, staff, and customers alike.

The first time I'd seen them, they were chanting slogans, shouting at the customers who tried to get through their blockade, and courting the attention of local media. Bad news for everyone involved. The owner eventually sold the place to someone else, who distanced the business from the previous guy's comments. Everyone seemed to calm down after that. But as the protesters' ire faded, they gradually transformed into something completely different: the local meet up of rowdy chess players.

There were about a dozen of them, as much regular patrons of the place as anyone else who sat inside. Having turned their protest signs into makeshift tables, the group's attention was devoted to the chess games happening atop them at any given time. I'm sure the new owners of Layla's Rumour could have had them removed for trespassing, but it seemed like their presence actually brought new business from the local chess fans. Or maybe they got used to each other's presence and settled on a stalemate.

"You sacrificed your queen!" one man shouted at the white player. His words travelled around a cigarette and through a salt-and-pepper goatee. "That's your most important piece."

"Shush," another observer said, this one with a blue baseball cap, "I've seen this one play before. She knows what she's doing."

"But why would she sacrifice her queen?" asked Goatee.

"Just shut up and watch, would ya?" said Ballcap.

White moved her rook to B6, putting the black king in check.

"Oh man, look at that!" Goatee grabbed my shoulders and jumped up and down in front of me. "Did you see that? Look, the king is in check and he can't take the rook because of her knight there."

"Yeah, wow," I said, though the game actually was more interesting than my lack of enthusiasm revealed. I resolved to stick around to the end of it.

Black responded to this move by moving his king to C8, taking the knight and getting out of check.

"Why does she keep sacrificing pieces?" said Goatee. "This lady has no idea what she's doing."

"Nope, it's all over now," said Ballcap. "White wins."

"Are you sure?" asked Goatee.

"Take a look, for god's sake. Quit yakking and think for a minute." Ballcap thumped on the side of Goatee's head. "The king is surrounded by his own pawns. He's not going to be able to get away. Watch, White is going to win on her next move."

"But Black has his queen covering him," said Goatee.

White moved her rook to B8, taking the king's pawn.

"Okay, so he's in check, so what," said Goatee.

"What are you asleep or something? Look at his bishop at G3. It has the rook covered." said Ballcap. "Black can't use his king to take White's rook without the bishop taking the king."

"Damn, you're right. It's checkmate!" shouted Goatee. "This lady is amazing!"

"Another round," Black said to White.

"No," said White. "You lose twice and we don't play again. That's the rule. "

"Let's go," another person said to Black, tapping him on the shoulder and motioning for the defeated player to take a hike. "You lost. I'm up next."

I left the chess club and entered the bar. It wasn't the most charming place in the world, but it was far from the least. A bit of a dad bar, I guess, but it had the benefit of being across the street from my condo so I didn't complain. I grabbed one of the few empty seats at the bar. I wasn't so much of a regular that everyone in the place recognized me, but at least the bartender did.

"Hey bud," he said, a peppy young guy with an absurdly fashionable haircut and a red jacket over a white shirt, a black bow tie restraining its butterfly collar. "The usual?"

I nodded.

He brought me a glass of their cheapest red wine, which I sipped as I watched the aloo football game on TV.

"I can't believe you bums want to sit around and watch robots play sports," I heard a barfly say a couple seats down from me, his brittle, gravelly voice no doubt the result of decades of chain smoking. "Why do they televise this garbage?"

The room erupted in cheers at a particular hit—one aloo football player had slammed into another one, shattering the first one clean in two and sending mechanical guts flying in every direction across the field.

"Did you see that?" asked another barfly beside Chain Smoker. His deep, booming foghorn of a voice was far louder than it needed to be—the chess players must have heard him outside. "You thought that was boring? That was awesome! It's like football mixed with a demolition derby."

"Yeah, but what happened to real athletes?" asked Chain Smoker. "What happened to actual people playing actual sports?"

"Those things are still remote controlled by actual players," said Foghorn. "Aloos aren't that quick yet. And this way it's safer but they can get even more violent. A hit like that would've killed a guy."

"Athletes! You call those guys athletes! They sit around in a chair playing football like it's a video game!"

"It's all fixed anyway," said a third voice, so nasal, so penetrating it nearly gave me an earache. "You see the way those parts went flying like that? Ain't no way it could've happened like that from that impact. I tell ya, those things are rigged to explode at the slightest touch."

"Man, you used to say real football games were rigged too," said Foghorn. "Everything's rigged to you!"

"Well yeah, because it is," said Earache.

Chain Smoker sighed. "I just want to watch a real football game in a bar with my pals," he muttered to his pint. "Is that too much to ask?"

"I tell you what Fitz," said Earache, "during the commercials we'll switch to the human football game, alright? But the rest of us like watching these robots destroy themselves. It's like football mixed with a demolition derby."

I stared aimlessly at the antiquated TVs hanging on the walls for a few minutes, watching as the aloo cleaners swept the remains of the felled player off the field. Earache was probably right—that thing was hit at the 30 yard line, and its guts were spread as far as the touchdown spot, whatever it's called—I never cared much for sports. Though I must admit, watching the aloos destroy each other was pretty cool.

"What do you think of aloo football, bud?" asked a guy beside me. "Pretty cool how those things destroy each other, huh?"

I noticed his breath before anything else. It smelled like a family of alcoholic skunks had died in his mouth three weeks ago. He didn't look much better.

"Yeah, it's great," I stifled my gag reflex.

"I don't think I seen you here before. Name's Dewey." He offered his hand.

"Auden," I said, returning the gesture.

"Nice to meet you, Auden. What did you do before you were bottom lined?"

This guy just automatically assumed I was bottom lined, I thought. *Is that where we're at now? Are we at the point where the average guy is bottom lined? Also, how could a living human being possibly produce a smell this horrible?*

"Uh, I still have a job actually. I'm a crane operator." I held my wine close to my nose.

"Well no kidding, good for you bud. I miss working. Been bottom lined for about a year. I was an auto mechanic, specialized in those Corvair aloo-cabs. Thought it was a steady job, since there are tons of those things around now. But they got aloos to fix them now. Aloos fixing aloos. Something… unnatural about it."

He took a long draw from his pint, swishing the beer around in his mouth for a moment and letting it mingle with the memories of his past life. Was he trying to sweeten the memories of a life with purpose, or hoping enough beer would drown them out forever?

"So uh, what do you do now?" I asked.

"You're looking at it." He turned back toward the bar, staring at nothing in particular.

"Are you looking for a way to spend your time?" said a voice from the television. I looked up to see a middle-aged guy in a grey business suit straight out of the 1980's on the screen, wearing a smile and haircut he must have removed from the refrigerator just before they shot this commercial.

On closer look, it may have been an aloo. Hard to tell. He was standing on the left side of the screen against a blue background. "Feeling bored, listless, uninterested in life? Is your spouse nagging you like crazy? Then this is one opportunity you won't want to miss!"

"Entroco has tens of thousands of positions available for people of all education levels, backgrounds, and skills. It doesn't matter what you did before," a list of obsolete careers scrolled by on the right side of the screen beside him. I was pretty sure I spotted construction worker in the list somewhere, but it moved so fast it was hard to tell. "So long as you're a hard worker, we have a place for you. To find out more, dial 1-811-555-7600, or visit us at www.Entroco.career. We need you!"

Of course. People always find meaning somehow, I thought. There must be loads of companies like Entroco out there, providing people with meaning in their life once again. I resolved to look into these Entroco guys once I was bottom lined. Though I doubted they'd have a crane operator job available, I figured I could learn to do something new. After all, what could they do, fire me if I did a bad job?

I should tell the other guys about this too. Especially Eddie, he'd be so happy to hear about this company and this opportunity. He could be happy again. So could the others, if they wanted to, I mean. Avery and Noble looked like they had a good thing going, but the other guys might want to know about this once they get bottom lined.

Hell, maybe I should tell the guys at head office about it. Guys could transition from working for Edcon to Entroco, if they wanted. For the guys who wanted to keep working, it would make them a lot happier. It would make them less stressed out, less anxious about their future. It would be perfect.

Yeah, I'll talk to Byron about telling head office. And I'll tell Eddie about it too.

"Hey you checked out that Entroco thing, right?" said Foghorn. "What was up with it?"

"It was a scam," said Earache. "They set it up to get as much of your personal information as they can so they can crack into your bank account and siphon all your cash into an offshore account. I nearly fell for it too."

"What made you stop?" asked Foghorn.

"It was weird as soon as I walked in the door. The lady never told me exactly what they did or answered any questions. She said something vague about foreign aid work or something. As soon as she asked for my bank information, I got up and walked out. She said they needed it so they could deposit my pay into my account, but there's no reason they need to know everything they had asked me to do that. I'm lucky I used to work in a bank, otherwise I probably would have fallen for it. They had a hell of a pitch."

"I can't believe they still let those ads on TV then," said Chain Smoker.

"I read they were getting investigated last week," said Earache. "I don't think we'll see them for much longer."

Well, there goes that idea.

I pulled out my phone and searched "jobs for bottom liners." Entroco may have been a scam, I reasoned, but someone must have come up with something for bottom liners to do. After the handful of ads at the top, including one for Entroco (I reported it as a scam) and a few Craigslist postings, I found a few more companies—Datamist, Futureland, Extentatech, and The Human Company— which all offered jobs to bottom liners.

Further research on www.ScamHamster.track, though, revealed each of these to be scams.

As if on cue, another commercial showed up on the screen.

"When we saw these people losing their jobs, losing their livelihoods, we realized we needed to do something about it," said the familiar voice of Prime Minister Karloff Durham over the sterile, cold rhythm of corporate stock audio soundtrack. I looked up to see him walking across a tranquil meadow, wildflowers growing all around him. "So we created the bottom line."

"The bottom line is a program to help displaced workers retain their lifestyle," a pleasant woman's voice said over a scene of a family frolicking in a park like you see in one of those commercials for the latest pharmaceutical drugs. "It provides those—"

"Enough of this," growled Chain Smoker as the television changed channels to the football game. "We all know about the bottom line. Let's watch some football players play some football!"

I gulped down the rest of my wine and went home.

# 12

Leopards don't hate gazelles, but we can be forgiven for thinking they do. As a leopard glares at a herd of gazelles from a pile of grass and branches, her eyes narrow. Her spots are a series of highways on a map all leading to her mouth, which, when opened, bares her deadly fangs. She picks out the closest, weakest member of the herd and arranges her hind legs appropriately. At the right moment, she bursts forth from the grass, racing toward her target. If she's lucky, she'll sink her teeth and claws into the gazelle's flesh, filling her belly and staving off the reaper for another day.

As soon as the herd notices the leopard, they flee, of course. Nobody wants to be someone else's lunch. But once the leopard catches its target and the rest of the herd notices their fallen family member, they stop running. After all, a leopard only kills when she's hungry.

The only motivation a leopard has for killing a gazelle is her own empty stomach. A leopard feasting on a fresh kill may be the ideal place for a gazelle to be, since the leopard's presence will scare off any lesser predators. Because the leopard behaves like this, there will always be enough gazelles for her to eat.

At least, that's what they said in the nature documentary I fell asleep watching last night.

Meanwhile, the gazelle population also doesn't hate grass, even though they pull it out and feast on it all day. They never tear out more grass than they need to eat at that time, and they return the favour by fertilizing the ground with their shit, which allows new grass to sprout up even healthier than before.

It's the closest thing to a perpetual motion machine out there. Everything works in harmony.

When newcomers show up in the environment, they need to be sensitive to this balance. If they can match the pace of everyone around them, order is maintained and the rest of the ecosystem can preserve its balance.

And if they're familiar with the flora and fauna of the region, they generally will. A travelling pride of lions, displaced by a natural disaster, will show up and feed on the same herd of gazelles the leopard does. The balance of power may shift. After a few pissing matches, the leopards and lions learn to respect each other's boundaries and coexist in an uneasy ceasefire that will last as long as the gazelles. Like new members of an orchestra, the lions will recognize the song being played and eke out their own part within the melody.

But if the newcomer to an ecosystem is completely foreign, it can cause all sorts of problems. Let's drop a grizzly bear into the middle of the savannah. Aeons of evolution have prepared leopards for dealing with lions and cheetahs and hyenas and I don't know, maybe pythons or rhinoceroses or whatever else preys on gazelles, but not for grizzly bears.

And the bears, likewise, are used to dealing with cougars and wolves and coyotes and other bears, and moose maybe, though I don't know if moose are carnivores, but I think you get the point. Neither knows what to do with the other. This foreign invader is deaf to the community melody, interrupting their carefully performed Bach symphony with atonal noise rock.

The only way to solve this imbalance is to remove the invader or accept it as the new top of the food chain and adjust to the new regime, usually at the expense of the previous residents.

In the ecosystem of our work savannah, the aloos were the grizzly bears. The only way Byron could keep the balance was by taking guys off the crew. Even with Eddie, Avery, and Noble gone, the aloos were still far ahead of everyone else. Either they or the remaining crew would end up sitting dormant for at least a couple hours a day while everyone else caught up.

And since aloos worked harder and more efficiently than humans did, and for free, the company decided to cut more of us.

They also sent us a new aloo. Instead of being human shaped like the others it was just a box that plugged into the ports on the backhoe to operate it, so we didn't bother giving it a name.

And unlike the others, Backhoe was one machine designed for one job to replace one guy. Along with Backhoe came orders to bottom line Keith along with three carpenters. Sticking with the same logic as last time, Byron chose Gael, Brynlee, and Kay.

Keith didn't react much one way or another to the news. Byron had told him before everyone else, hoping to avoid another scene. But Keith wasn't far from retirement anyway, so to him it was more like a get out of jail free card a few years early.

Byron talked to Gael, Kay, and Brynlee separately from Keith as well, and they were all fine with it too. Instead of cutting them off that day, he gave them the option of staying on for another month on a part time basis to ease the transition, but they declined. I guess it was better to rip the bandage off than peel it away slowly.

Without them, the four aloos had the responsibility of seven carpenters and a backhoe, but they were still far ahead of schedule. After all, they worked 18+ hours a day and the rest of us needed time to relax.

It was a matter of time before more of us were replaced, but there was no word on a crane operator aloo yet, so at least for now I was safe.

We hit The Black Cat to celebrate everyone's last day, which was starting to become a tradition. Avery and Noble joined us as well.

"Where's Eddie? Either of you seen him?" Keith asked, as if they were all a part of each other's daily lives now that they were all bottom liners. But they hadn't seen him. Nobody had since the last time we were all there together. Several of us tried to invite him out (I hadn't, but you've probably guessed by now that I wasn't exactly the social hub of the crew) before tonight, without any response.

"I saw him the other day," Arya poured another pint. "Poor guy was so drunk he could barely stand. I had to call him a cab home."

"Did he say anything?" asked Mateah.

"Not much. I didn't even serve him. He was plastered the moment he came in. He complained about aloos, declared his love for me, you know, typical drunk guy stuff. He was especially pissed off that I called him an aloo cab—said I should have called a 'real' cab with a 'real' person driving it. As if there are any of those out there anymore. But he didn't look good. Like he's been drunk more often than sober lately."

"Poor guy," said Avery.

The air hung heavily for a long moment. I had just mentally boarded an airplane to South America when Brynlee cracked the silence.

"So tell me guys," he said to Avery and Noble, "what can I expect now that I'm one of you?"

Noble piped up immediately. "I got a LifeSim, so I spend a lot of time in there. I'm living with the lizard people on Kurtadam."

"Whoa, whoa, whoa, hang on Noble," said Gael. "The lizard people? What are you talking about?"

"Oh, uh, it's a game," said Noble as he shifted his posture. "Haven't you heard of the LifeSim? It's a simulator that reproduces all five senses in your body. Lately I've been playing Vast, and it feels like it's all real. You look at the twin suns setting over the ocean, and it looks like a real sunset. You can hear the waves lapping against the shore, smell the salt water brine, and even taste the food. My character is a lizard person from the planet Kurtadam, and it actually feels like I'm a lizard. If I touch my arm I can feel the scales on it. It's so surreal."

"That game's pretty good," said Mateah. "A friend of mine helped develop it. I usually spend my time on a different sector of the galaxy, but if I'm ever near Kurtadam I'll give you a shout. Send me your username?"

Noble smiled and nodded, and the two of them exchanged information.

"You're in the LifeSim too?" asked Arya. "It's so much fun! I tried one with my friend last weekend, and we had an amazing time. I'm going to get one soon too. Maybe I'll come visit you. But I don't think I want to be a lizard girl."

"Yeah, that sounds weird, man," Gael shook his head.

"Well, maybe a little bit... but it's fun. I built my own house along the shore of the Krozagrumg Ocean. The breeze feels amazing, and you should see how the double sunset lights up the remzelks floating on the ocean. It's the most spectacular thing you can imagine."

"It lights up the what?" asked Avery.

"The remzelks," Noble shifted in his chair. "They're like, algae I guess. They float on the ocean near where my house is. I mean, my house in Vast, heh."

"So let me get this straight," said Gael after a brief pause. "You're in, like, a frog simulator? You spend all your time pretending you're a frog?"

"I am definitely not going to miss you, Gael." Mateah shook her head and took a long drink from her pint.

"Not a frog, a lizard. And no, not all the time. There's all sorts of simulations. You can be the pilot of a jet fighter, a Roman soldier, whatever you want. You can even have jobs in the sims too. You can meet up with anyone else in the same sim, call people outside of it, hook up with all sorts of alien babes, or even be one of the alien babes if you want. You can do whatever you want and it feels like you're actually there. It's amazing."

"They're training you for the inevitable reptilian takeover, you fool! Can't you see that? They're trying to get you used to the idea of seeing lizards everywhere, which will make it that much easier once they reveal their plan to enslave us all. Don't you people ever use your brains?"

Brynlee pursed his lips. "You know Draven, did you ever consider why no one listens to you is because all you talk about is crazy shit? Don't you have any other interests other than the reptilians and the new world order?"

"It's not crazy shit, it's important shit and no one seems to care about it! I have to talk about it! If I don't, who will?"

"But look, we've worked together for, what, twelve years now? And I don't know nothin' about you. I don't even know if you're married or not. Don't you think that's weird? Why don't you try talking about something else for once?"

"Shut up for a minute, you two," Karter shoved the two aside. "So you mean you can go into this thing and create whatever body you want for yourself?"

"Yeah, that's the way it works man," said Noble.

"And it feels like it's real?"

"As real as real life."

"Think I could uh, come by and give it a try some time?" Karter looked down at his legs; they were shaped more like a cat's hind legs than a human's, and gave him an unnatural bounce with each step he took. That made them more effective, but it also made it painfully obvious that they were artificial. "It would be nice to feel what it's like to have real legs again."

"Yeah, sure man. I got an extra input for it for two players. You've got my number. Give me a shout. I've got a hell of a lot of spare time these days. I'm sure you will too, soon enough."

"... Alright, so Noble spends his time pretending to be an alien frog babe," said Gael with a raised eyebrow. "What about you, Avery?"

"Asshole," Noble muttered under his breath. That sort of reaction was exactly why I never told anyone about what I did all day in the crane. But I did like the sound of that LifeSim thing. It didn't sound much different than what I liked to do anyway. Maybe Noble and I, and Mateah and Arya too, had more in common than I thought.

Avery stretched his arms across the back of the booth where he sat. "My days are full. Usually I wake up around noon, eat some breakfast, then I watch some TV for a while. Might play a game or two. Then I meet up with a couple friends for dinner, we hit a club for the night, and party hard. Good times man, good times."

Avery was never a slim guy, but he'd noticeably gained pudge since I last saw him. Given what he'd told us, I wasn't surprised. The youngest other than Gill and Noble, he hadn't seen the years of hard work that had worn the rest of us down (though neither had I—years of sitting in the crane left me with more delicate hands than the others, but it hadn't exactly done wonders for my waistline either).

"You're lucky you hit the bottom line at your age," said Leopold. "I wish I could have retired at 28. I'm sure I'll spend most of my time at home with Ahmed getting my ear nagged off."

"You're not that old, you know. There's a lot you could do with a bottom line lifestyle once you're here. You could even join us one night at a club. Give you a chance to take your mind off things and just have a little fun. You might even meet someone new."

"I would never cheat on Ahmed," Leopold said, with as much indignation as I've seen anyone muster. "He's my rock and my life. I don't know what I'd do without him."

I cringed.

"So how come all you do is complain about him?" Clearly Avery had opened up a topic he shouldn't have, but it was too late to go back now.

Leopold sighed. "I guess I do give that impression, don't I? We can be hard on each other, but he's not so bad. Ahmed was bottom lined a few years ago, so he's had some time to fill his schedule with new things to do and we don't see each other very often. But I have no idea what I'll do, so I'm picturing us getting in each other's hair all the time and driving each other nuts. It'll probably be fine. I'm being dramatic, I don't know. You'll probably understand if you ever get married."

"Yeah, I think I know what you mean," said Noble. "I'm not married, but I do have a roommate and we get in each other's way sometimes. Before it was no big deal since he worked nights, but now that I'm around during the day he gets annoyed that I'm in the house during what used to be his quiet time. That's part of why the LifeSim is so appealing. But Ahmed found stuff to do, right? So you probably will too."

"I'd be annoyed if my roommate spent all day pretending to be an alien frog babe all day too."

"You're such a dick, Gael. Piss off, alright?"

"Whatever, weirdo."

"Don't let him get under your skin," said Mateah. "It's not his fault he was born with absolutely no good qualities whatsoever."

"Watch your mouth Mateah." Gael made himself as large as he could. "Just because you're a woman doesn't mean I can't knock you out. Equality right? Isn't that what all you feminists are always on about?"

"I'd like to see you try it," Mateah inflated herself similarly.

"So what do you like to do anyway, Leopold?" Karter changed the subject.

"I've been thinking about that more lately. Trying to remember what I used to like doing when I was younger."

"And?"

"I don't know. I'm drawing a blank. I mean, like, comic books and action figures, but that's stuff for kids, not for a grown man."

"Why not? Noble spends all his time in the frog simulator and Brynlee just plays Pac Man all day, so why can't you read comic books?" asked Gael.

"Fuck you, Gael," said Noble. "What are you going to do then that's so amazing?"

"I'm not going to live in the land of make believe like you losers," he rested his forearm on the back of his chair. "How can any of you call yourselves adults and respect yourselves if you pretend to be a cartoon character all day?"

"Answer the question, asshole," Noble leaned in, fists clenched. "What are you going to do with your time?"

"I haven't figured it out yet. But I'm sure it will be more interesting than playing make believe all day like little children."

"Geez, is this what I get to look forward to?" asked Leopold, both trying to defuse the tension and asking the question that was doubtless on everyone's minds.

"Not necessarily," said Kay. "I'm actually really happy. It will give me more time to devote to my art."

"What kind of art?" asked Brynlee.

"You didn't know she was an artist?" asked Gill. "Shit, even I knew that."

"Yeah, I'm a 3D environment modeller. Digital worlds and stuff. The kind of worlds you'd be exploring in your LifeSim actually."

"So nobody wants to live in reality anymore," Gael walked off toward the washroom. "Bunch of weirdos."

"I'm happy doing what I do," said Kay. "And that's all that matters."

I guess she's right. But was Gael totally wrong too? Noble and Avery seemed to be doing alright, but I don't think they'd really figured it out yet. And everyone else's reactions ranged from quiet excitement to downright anxiety.

But we were the lucky ones, right?

There've been hundreds of millions of humans throughout history who would have committed unspeakable acts to trade places with any one of us. Even if I was never replaced, the fact I could consider the possibility of a labour-free life without enslaving thousands to do my bidding meant I had it better than almost anyone who ever lived.

When I was in high school, our history teacher gave us an essay to write. He gave us the number of pages and sources he wanted, which was pretty typical. He also said we could write it about anything we wanted, which was exciting. The mind-blowing part, though, was that we weren't allowed to use a computer at all in creating it.

Writing without a computer? Research without the internet? Impossible! Ridiculous! Absurd! How could we possibly find the information we were looking for?

My 14-year-old mind couldn't have been more shocked if I had gone to sleep in my bed and woken up naked and tied to a wooden raft floating down a river in the middle of a jungle, covered in honey and swarmed by bees. A few class members shrieked in horror. One kid dropped dead of a heart attack. All the lights in the room went dark except for a spotlight which shone on the teacher from directly above as he laughed maniacally like a super villain revealing his evil plan of world domination to the United Nations.

I might be misremembering that a bit.

I told my dad about it, whose laughter was the perfect antidote to my panicked delirium. To my surprise, that's how he'd done most of his assignments until the internet had really taken off in his late teens.

That's when it hit me: my dad was older than the internet.

Okay yeah, the internet was invented in the 1960s as a spy communication network and blah, blah, blah. Until the 1990s, the only people who knew about it viewed it on green and black screens through smudged and broken glasses from inside a pair of khaki shorts, Velcro sandals atop white tube socks, and a wrinkled polo shirt with a pocket protector. And since my dad was born in the 1980s and never wore a pocket protector (I think), he remembered life before the internet.

He then began to paint a picture of what life was like back when he was a kid. Back in the dark ages. Apparently they had only one phone number for the whole house, and if you wanted to connect to the internet, you couldn't use the phone anymore and it would make this horrible sound to connect.

If someone needed to use the phone, you had to disconnect so they could do it, and if someone called on the phone, your connection dropped even if you were in the middle of a game or an important conversation with your internet crush.

Between not having the internet, then crummy internet, then getting bottom lined before the bottom line was a thing (how trendy of him), my dad's generation struggled a lot more than mine did.

They were the in between generation, stuck with the burden of the economic, environmental, and social mismanagement of their parents' generation and left to fix it with the meagre resources that weren't being hoarded by the people who had created the problem in the first place.

Most of them didn't have any kids of their own until well into their forties, if at all, and as a result, the rate of birth defects skyrocketed.

To my dad's dad, though, his struggle would have seemed quaint, childish, almost adorable. Having grown up and lived the prime of his life in the economically and culturally affluent 1960s to the '90s, would my grandfather's generation have faced the same existential crises we do today?

And what about his parents and grandparents? Baptized in the nightmare of the First and Second World Wars, what would they think of being handed a life of zero responsibility?

I've watched documentaries about the 1940s and '50s, where the soldiers came back from WWII and settled into what seems like a boring, unfulfilling civilian life.

They left their minds where they hung their jackets, as they signed in to work in an office or industrial job from the time they returned from Europe or Asia until the day they retired in their suburban houses. As generic as the ones 3D printers hammer out these days.

Maybe after six years of hell, a quiet, predictable family life was enough for them. Maybe they were just grateful to not get shot at and not have their friends die in their arms on a weekly basis. Maybe they were so shaken from post-traumatic stress that they could barely handle anything else.

They likely would have considered us lazy and entitled, just like every older generation does the younger. It always seems that way, a combination of viewing the past through the lens of nostalgia and a tendency to scoff at things we don't understand.

When archaeologists try to translate a newly discovered ancient language, "kids these days" must be the standard phrase they start with.

I've never experienced anything that terrible. The worst I've dealt with was the stress of my undergrad, the first time I climbed up into the crane, and having to put my blind, deaf, toothless old family dog down. I've never even seen a real gun outside a museum, let alone been shot at. I've never been in a fight before, not even a childhood scuffle on the playground.

And while I might imagine myself as a soldier in the Trojan War, the American Civil War, or any of dozens of other conflicts, all I'm doing is living in a land of make believe. I have no better understanding of what it was actually like in those situations than someone who's watched a movie.

But that's what almost every human throughout history has to face.

Our generation is soft, I guess. I mean, sure, there's still a military. And there is still conflict. But you're more likely to be injured in the Disaster Assistance Force they created a couple decades ago than the military these days. And since most of the more dangerous jobs in the DAF are being done by aloos anyway, the point is kind of moot.

I guess it's the hero's journey that makes the reward that much sweeter. Would Odysseus have appreciated his homecoming as much if he hadn't spent twenty years away?

"Hello Odysseus, welcome to Troy," King Priam would say as he rolled out a plush carpet. "Yes, please come out. We've gone ahead and destroyed the city for you, and returned Helen to Menelaus. I hope it wasn't too much trouble for you to come here. Oh, and we've cleared the seas for you to get home, too—you and your men will have a smooth journey. Poseidon has already agreed to this. He won't cause any problems. In fact, he's prepared a feast for you all. I'm sure you're anxious to get home, only take your time—the ambrosia we have for you is exquisite, having been prepared by Zeus himself, and we'd hate for you to rush through it. Oh, and the men who were thinking of courting your wife have all been killed and dumped into the sea. Everything's taken care of. Sorry to have made you come this far for nothing. Cheers, let me know if there's anything else we can do to help."

Somehow it doesn't seem as great.

But that's the life our children will be gifted with. If I ever have a child (which looks unlikely at this point), they'll never have to work a day in their life. We won't need them at all, probably. I mean, maybe they'll become writers or musicians or painters or comedians, but we definitely won't need to train them to be lawyers or doctors or crane operators.

And when we tell them stories about our lives, we'll tell them about how we used to have to work to make a living, and they will gasp in horror and disbelief. Work for your money? Impossible! Ridiculous! Absurd! Where would you find time for yourself if you worked 8 hours a day!?

"Auden, are you coming or what?"

Oh geez, I'd done it again.

# 13

The following Monday, those of us who still had a job showed up to find Byron and Lyla Maddox, our liaison from head office, having a chat with a tall, thin man in an expensive suit. The emblem embossed on his briefcase was the same as the one on our aloos' shoulders: Eris Industries.

His meticulously blow dried and parted black hair matched the colour of his business suit, which looked pristine and polished in the same way a section of carpet you vacuumed and shampooed would look if the rest of it were still buried in dirt. Under his arm he carried a shiny hard hat with the residue of a price tag sticker on it, which he reluctantly put on after an inaudible comment from Byron.

Lyla's hard hat reflected the fact that she worked for a construction company and had been to a few job sites. But her outfit reflected that she worked for a construction company in its air conditioned corporate office downtown. Byron, meanwhile, looked as grimy as the rest of us. The three of them were standing beside Byron's office trailer, all circled around our growing family of aloos.

Before I had time to wonder what they were talking about, a loud clanging echoed from behind me. I turned around to see an avalanche of pipes, out from which a figure began to emerge. Just another homeless wanderer, I figured.

"Byron! Byron!" our foreman's name hurled in every direction, a blind volley that stained everyone in sight with the stench of sweat and cheap liquor. His face was obscured by unkempt hair and a patchy beard in which he stored the remnants of a recent meal, some of which had migrated to his shirt—the same shirt he had worn the last time I saw him nearly a month earlier.

His eyes were like craters on the dark side of the Moon; black, lifeless holes in a lifeless rock.

Still, it was unmistakably Eddie.

"Byron, where are ya, I got a, a, whatchacallit, a plan, no, a, propuhsishun fer ya!" he shouted as he regained his balance. Byron, mortified, excused himself to tend to Eddie.

"Eddie, what the hell are you doing here?"

"G'mornin Byron," he slurred, snapping himself to stand up straight like a green soldier in basic training or a wet noodle slapped down on a table. His voice then dropped to a back alley, conspiratorial, hey kid, you wanna buy a watch whisper. "I wass hopin' yous going to do some work, er, going to lemme do some work, you gotta job fer me?"

"Eddie, I'm sorry, there's no more work for you here. We just let Keith, Gael, and Brynlee go recently and—"

"See thassa problem here. Yer lettin everyone go man, wass we sposta do then, huh? Wass we sposta do?" A finger-jab to Byron's chest punctuated each word of the last sentence.

"That's up to you Eddie. Why don't we—"

"I know iss up t'me!" Eddie shouted as he paced, hurling his arms into the air with such force that they would have landed on the building's third floor had they not been anchored to his shoulders. "Thass what everyone sez man, sez I gotta figger it out." After a moment, he dropped his tone again and continued.

"Look man, Byron, I'm fucked up man, no jobs or nothin', nothin' to do, nothing to work fer, I got nothin' man, I mississ place, workin with you guys, man," he turned and looked at the growing group of us. "You Sam, yous always a good one, an Draven yous a weirdo but yous a good one, even you Auden." He pointed at me and walked toward me. "Even though youss kinda a dick t'everyone, youss a good guy man, youss a good guy, don't ferget it, don't, man enjoy workin' here man, iss shit out there. They's going to replace ya soon man, all youss going to be replaced and yer life's gonna be shit man, no one needs ya, no one needs no one for nothin no more..."

As he trailed off, Byron put his hand on Eddie's shoulder. "Come on Eddie, let's get you a coffee and call you a ride home." He led Eddie off to the food printer.

"Iss those robots man, life's been shit since those things came up" he said, pointing at Hank as they walked. "Got no purpose now man... Hey Lyla, whass u doin' here lookin' all sexy, whass you doin' here?" he did an obnoxious little dance. Lyla rolled her eyes.

"An whass yer deal suit man? You from the FBI or somethin'?" Eddie slapped his knee, cackling. "Lookit yer suit man, secret agent shit man, an lookit yer suitcase, briefcase, man, whass this fuckin' guy, you gonna investigate some secret shit man, talk to Draven man, he knows all the secret shit."

Before Draven had a chance to respond to this sudden light shone on his anti establishment activities, a light switch in Eddie's mind turned his expression from jovial to black. "Hey juss a minute... That suitcase on yer... Yer from that fuckin' robot fuckers took my job! You ruined my fuckin' life!"

Eddie shook Byron off and ran toward the Eris rep. Horrified, the Eris rep began to run up the three stairs to Byron's office trailer. Lyla followed him and stood at the bottom of the stairs like a football player to try and stop Eddie, but he easily bucked her aside. As the Eris rep fiddled with the doorknob trying to open the door, Eddie caught up to him and slammed into the man's back, splattering him against the door.

The force of the impact bounced Eddie back far enough for him to swing his fist around like a crane arm, hitting the Eris rep square in the jaw and knocking him over the edge of the handrail before himself tumbling backward down the stairs.

Both hit the ground like bags of sand. As the Eris rep clawed dazed at the ground, Eddie climbed back up the stairs and leapt over the railing after him, landing on the Eris rep's stomach and clamping his hands around his throat.

Lyla brought herself to her feet and joined the struggle, trying to peel Eddie's hands away, but he was a threatened animal with a single minded commitment to the destruction of what had hurt him; channelling every moment of despair he'd experienced in the weeks since he was bottom lined into his grip around the Eris rep's throat.

Karter's artificial legs allowed him to catch up to the chaos before anyone else did. He grabbed Eddie's shoulders to try and pull him back, but even with Lyla's help it was no good.

The Eris rep flailed about, his face turning blue as he gasped for air under Eddie's gorilla grip. He pounded against Eddie's chest and swung impotently at him, catching him square in the jaw with a few weak punches, each of which served only to make Eddie angrier.

It wasn't until Byron, Draven, and Mateah caught up that the five of them were able to make progress. They peeled Eddie's fingers away one by one as the Eris rep's resistance faded and his body began to go limp. Once they finally pulled his hands back, the rep took his first unrestricted gasp of air, but the reprieve lasted only a second.

Eddie grabbed the man's tie as they pulled him away. The Eris rep was dragged along the ground like a stubborn dog before the four of them stopped pulling, and Lyla loosened the tie enough for the man to slip out of it. They dragged Eddie, struggling, screaming and gyrating, to Byron's office and slammed the door shut.

Lyla was left behind, shaken and startled. She did her best to help the Eris rep to his feet, but the heel she was counting on her left shoe snapped off in the struggle. She staggered backward, which caused the Eris rep to lose his balance. The two fell in a crumpled heap.

"You, call an ambulance!" Lyla shouted from beneath the Eris rep as she pointed to Sam with a well manicured but dirt covered finger.

"You," she pointed to Gill, who was arriving to work for the morning, "help me out here!"

Gill raced over, confused, to help Lyla and the Eris rep to their feet.

"You!" she pointed to Kay. "Get the first aid kit!"

She and Gill helped the Eris rep to his feet and seated him on a pile of material, Lyla limping along and filling the air with apologies.

I stood there like an idiot, listening to Eddie's muffled screams from within the trailer.

After a moment, Byron emerged from the office. "I need everyone to get to work. We'll talk about this later."

To Byron, later usually meant never, but I had a feeling this was one issue he couldn't avoid.

While the rest of the crew dealt with the situation at hand, I made my way over to the crane.

# 14

"How much to get to The Hall?"

I sat at a circular table across from a captain of a cargo ship. She hadn't given me her name, and when I pressed, she gave me only a single letter: K. Her eyes were dark and sunken, face cracked and grizzled, no doubt a result of the salty sea air and a few hundred too many hours under the hot sun.

She wore a jacket that resembled an old confederate army uniform from 200 years ago. It looked about that old too, more patches than original material at this point.

She was the fifth captain I had spoken with thus far.

"Are you kidding?" K's voice was like tanned leather. "Unless The Council invites you, that place is a death trap. And if you're asking me for passage, they didn't invite you."

"I don't care," I said. "Can you take me there or not?"

"It'll cost you. A lot."

"I know. I just asked you the price. Quit stalling."

K leaned forward in her chair. "Alright look, it's a rough scene there. The Hall isn't a big fan of unwelcome solicitors. They shoot anyone who comes within range they don't recognize. That's where I got this." The captain pulled up her right sleeve to reveal a constellation of bullet wounds tracing a line halfway up her forearm. "The best I can do is to take you to the Echo Park flotilla. They send shipments to The Hall all the time. You can hire one of those ships from there. Any closer would be suicide. $400, paid up front."

The last two captains wanted $500.

"$350 and we're golden."

"This isn't a flea market, friend. $400, take it or leave it."

I hesitated a moment. "Alright, I'll take it."

"Great. Meet me at the Primm seaport. You know how to get there?"

"Yeah, it's southwest of here, right?"

"More or less. My ship is in bay 15. It's called The Refuge."

"15," I repeated.

"Why do you want to go there, anyway?" K asked. "Got a death wish or something?"

"Or something," I said. "It's probably best that you don't know the answer to that question."

"You're probably right," said K. She walked away without another word.

I returned to my coffee, pulling it toward me for a sip, then pushing it back. Why did the people who built the Echo Park Flotilla called it a flotilla when it wasn't a flotilla at all, but more of a stationary barge about the size of a city block. Maybe it was because "Echo Park Barge" doesn't sound quite as nice. Oh well, whatever. Not my concern.

I never liked this place. Just about everything was yellow, from the tobacco-stained ceiling to the rag in the bartender's hand and the teeth in his mouth. It was the kind of seedy hole that seemed to attract the lowest dregs of society. But most of the local captains loved the Bellagio, and I needed a captain.

When they weren't running cargo or passengers, most of the area's sailors made their way here to Vegas. Those who could afford it, anyway. The poorer ones stayed poor in Primm at the lower level casinos as they gambled away their meagre earnings.

All around me, people wasting their lives. Blackjack, roulette, poker, slots, it doesn't matter. It's all designed to extract as much money from you as possible while still giving you the illusion that you can win, and these suckers keep falling for it. Even the ones who do win just end up pissing their winnings away trying to get more. It's legalized theft, nothing more.

Not that I have anything against gambling. I love to gamble. Just not like these poor bastards in here. They're not going to get anywhere.

Take this drunk that just stumbled in here. I'm sure he drank away all his money at this point. It's 8 in the morning and he's already hammered. Maybe still hammered from the night before, who knows.

Look at him stumbling around and shouting at anyone who will listen, all the while the other patrons do their best to pay attention to their drinks and nothing else. I hope he doesn't come badger me.

Look at him running toward those people. What the hell does he think he's doing?

Look at him tackling that man like an animal. I don't think he even knows who the man is.

Look at him strangling that man, at the man gasping for air.

Look at the Eris rep struggling for air.

Look at Eddie strangling the Eris rep.

Look at Lyla trying to stop him.

Look at Karter trying to stop him.

Look at Byron trying to stop him.

Look at Draven trying to stop him.

Look at them dragging Eddie away.

Look at me.

Doing nothing.

Shit.

"Hey Auden, how are things up in the clouds today?"

Thank god, Sam. This was the fourth time I'd tried that today, and believe it or not it was the most successful attempt.

"Today hasn't been the best day so far. It's hard to concentrate."

"I know. The entire crew is out of sorts today. They're more efficient than usual, but I think that's because everyone is trying to distract themselves."

"How is the Eris guy doing?"

"I heard Byron call him Horkos, George Horkos. The paramedic said he has a concussion and a broken collarbone at very least, and might have gotten brain damage from the lack of oxygen and all the blows to his head. Poor guy. And Eddie too. I've never seen him like that. He wasn't happy about being bottom lined, but I didn't think it was that bad. I mean, I didn't think Eddie was a violent sort of guy, you know? I've never seen someone do something like that, attack someone out of nowhere, totally unprovoked. Have you?"

"No, not at all. He always seemed so easy going."

"Do you think the other guys are like that too? Like, do you think Avery and Noble are going to show up? Maybe we should hire a security guard for the site or something?"

"Hire a guy to protect us from the guys you fired? Seems, I don't know, backwards. Why not hire Eddie back?"

"That's obviously not going to happen now. But maybe Avery or Noble would want a job?"

"I don't know... I guess they have something else to fill their time with. Avery likes to party and drink, Noble is, uh, in a frog simulator I think." I silently cursed myself for repeating Gael's stupid insults.

"What the hell is a frog simulator?"

"I, uh, don't know, heh. You should ask Noble, maybe. Anyway, I'm sure the other guys are still doing what they love too. But I sat with Eddie for most of the night at the bar a few weeks back. He told me about his family, how they were all lazy and he was proud to have a job. He didn't want to end up a leech like them."

"But it's different if you're bottom lined. It's because you paid your dues, and society doesn't need you to work anymore."

"That's what I told him. Arya said the same thing too, but Eddie doesn't see it that way. Obviously, it was too much for him to bear. Anyway, is Lyla okay?"

"Yeah, she's fine. A couple cuts and bruises, but nothing major. She's pretty shaken up, though. I don't think she's used to dealing with situations like that."

"She handled it pretty well though, the way she took charge of things."

"She's a natural leader, so her instincts kicked in. But that doesn't mean it wasn't stressful. How often do you think they get drunks showing up and attacking people up at head office?"

"Yeah, true. So what do you think will happen to Eddie?"

"Horkos is definitely going to press charges, and even if he didn't, I'm sure Eris will. It doesn't look good, man. Eddie attacked someone unprovoked while drunk out of his mind at seven in the morning with at least a dozen witnesses. Byron called the police to deal with it. They'll be here any moment to take Eddie away, and they'll probably want statements from us. Byron and Lyla are going to get everyone caught up on what's going on. You should make your way down here."

"He called the cops on Eddie?"

"He had no choice. The cops would have found out from Horkos anyway. If they found out Byron let Eddie go without saying anything, he could be in trouble. We all could. I don't like it any more than you do, but Byron made the right decision."

"I can't believe it," I shook my head. Though the gesture was lost on Sam, I think he understood. "A couple months ago, everything was the same as it's always been, and now we're all being replaced, an innocent guy is badly hurt, and Eddie is going to jail."

"I know Auden. Everything is messed up. Just get down here, and we'll take care of it."

Byron and Lyla were standing together with a short, stocky police officer near Byron's trailer. Lyla had changed out of her ruined clothes and into what looked like a gym outfit, which must have been the only extra set of clothes she had with her at the time.

She had a square piece of gauze taped on her left forearm, a smaller bandage on her cheek, and more than a few scuffs and bruises on her legs. Despite all that, she stood a little taller than usual, trying to let us know things were under control. Byron began to speak.

"This morning, we were all witness to one of the worst things to ever happen to this crew. In case you weren't there, Lyla and I was meetin' with a guy from Eris Industries named George Horkos. He was here to check up on how the new aloos was treatin' us. He would have given all of them a check and told us how to make 'em work more efficient like, but he never got the chance."

"Shortly after we began the discussion," said Lyla, "a former colleague of yours, by the name of Mr. Edwin Hallstrom, arrived."

*Who? Oh, Eddie.*

"Mr. Hallstrom was intoxicated, and after causing a brief disturbance, attacked Mr. Horkos seemingly unprovoked."

"Eddie has been taken into police custody," said Byron. As if to pre-empt any objection, Byron waved his hand and explained. "I don't feel any better about it than any of you do. But we didn't have no choice."

"We're not sure what he's facing yet," said Lyla, "and we don't fully understand what happened. But the police have requested anyone who was present provide a statement on what you saw and what your relationship was like with Mr. Hallstrom. Officer Bielak here will take each of your—"

"Mr. George Horkos has been taken to Mt. Sinai Memorial Hospital and was admitted to the trauma unit," Bielak interrupted. He looked up at his forehead, speaking as though he were reciting sounds from pure memory without fully comprehending them, like an actor reading parts in a play in a language he didn't understand. "His injuries have been described as life threatening and he remains in critical condition. The medical team at Mt. Sinai remain optimistic about his pronglosis."

His what?

"Err, thanks officer," said Lyla. "Also, I'd like to thank Karter Lewis and Draven Garcia for your help in restraining Mr. Hallstrom. Your quick action today may have saved a man's life. And thanks, as well to Gillespie Chan, Samuel Soyinka, and Mateah Eccleston, who helped me tend to Mr. Horkos' injuries before the paramedics arrived. The police have been informed that while Edcon will do everything we can to facilitate Mr. Horkos' safety and recovery, and will cooperate with any investigation conducted, we cannot be held liable for Mr. Hallstrom's actions, since he is not in any way an agent or representative of Edcon, and was in fact already committing the criminal act of trespassing at the time of the assault."

"Whoa, hold on a minute," said Karter. "You're just throwing Eddie under the bus?"

"Let me handle this," Byron said to Lyla. "I ain't got no choice here. It's either Eddie gets what's comin' to him for what he did, or the rest of us face charges for covering up evidence of a crime. I don't know what Horkos is going to do, but if he doesn't press charges I'm sure Eris will. And if it comes out that we didn't give no statements and tried to cover up evidence, all of us could be in some deep shit. Eddie don't work here no more, so he doesn't get no special treatment."

"But how can you—" Karter began.

"Look, we all worked with Eddie a long time," Byron cut Karter off. "I knew him for longer than any of you. I grew up with the guy—we were neighbours when we were kids. And believe me, I'm doin' everything I can to help him out here. But he did what he did and ain't none of us can change that. I gotta protect all y'all too.

"After you give your statement, take the rest of the day off. Go home, clear your head, and let's come back tomorrow and get back to it."

"Hey Auden," Mateah asked me as I walked toward the subway, "Kay's going to come meet me for lunch. Do you want to come with us? That was really messed up, and we probably shouldn't be alone."

"Um, no thanks," I think I muttered as I shuffled away.

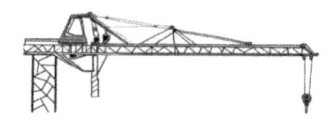

I lay in bed that night, reliving the day's events over and over as vividly as when it had happened that morning.

After what seemed like hours, my eyes opened without any of that characteristic heaviness you'd expect after trying to sleep. The red shine of my clock radio told me it was 1:13 a.m. Every morning I woke up amazed the thing still worked. It must be almost a century old—one of the few things of my dad's I took after he passed away.

Sleep wasn't going to be my friend that night, so I pulled on some clothes and went for a walk.

The moonless, cloudless sky, mostly obscured by the skyscraper condos and office buildings along Queen Street West, was completely black. Ambient light from the buildings provided a faint illumination, bolstered by the harsh blue glow of the halogen streetlights that stabbed at my eyes, accustomed as they were to the darkness of my bedroom a few moments ago.

These lights dotted the path before me, which brightened as I stepped within their motion sensors, and dimmed as I walked away—a new system implemented to save electricity when nobody was nearby.

There was a gap between the point where you exited the sensor area of the last light and entered the area of the next, which meant the light would oscillate. A hypnotizing cycle of bright, then dim, bright, then dim, swinging back and forth like a pendulum on a grandfather clock. They probably could make the light stay on just a second longer to prevent this.

Should I have done something differently? Should I have run in between Eddie and Horkos? Being realistic, there's no way I would have been able to stop Eddie. He spent all day banging hammers and lifting heavy things, and I spent all day sitting in a chair not lifting or doing anything, really. I wouldn't have been any more helpful than Lyla was.

*Bright.*

But Lyla was helpful, after all. She helped Horkos after the event, and she still played a role in getting Eddie free. I could have done something. But maybe I'd have gotten in the way. What if I had shouted something? Yeah, I should have shouted something. That would have made a difference.

*Dim.*

But what?

"Stop him!"

Lyla was already doing that. Then Karter. Then Byron, Mateah, and Draven. And they didn't do it in time anyway.

"Eddie, don't do it!"

Eddie wouldn't have heard me. And if he had, he wouldn't have cared. He wasn't even Eddie at that moment. He was out of his mind. And how could I have even known what sort of "it" Eddie was about to "do" anyway?

*Bright.*

"Horkos, look out!"

I didn't even know his name was Horkos at the time, so there goes that idea. And how exactly would he have "looked out" anyway? He had done that already by trying to duck into Byron's office, which had been locked. An extra half-second warning from me wouldn't have done anything.

*Dim.*

"Byron's trailer is locked! Run into the food trailer!"

Why would I have said that? I didn't know Byron's trailer was locked. And even if I had, he wouldn't have reacted in time. And even if he had, it wouldn't exactly have taken Hercules to rip the food trailer's door off its duct-tape hinges. It kept the rain out, and that's about it.

*Bright.*

I could have tried pulling Eddie away from Horkos like the rest, but I wouldn't have stood a chance. If Karter, Lyla, Draven, Byron, and Mateah together could barely pull Eddie away, there's no way I would have made a difference. It might have made me feel a little better knowing I'd done something more than, you know, nothing at all, but the outcome would have been the same.

The only way I could have made any difference would be if I had the clairvoyance to see what Eddie was about to do. I could have walked with Byron and Eddie and guided them in another direction, or asked Horkos to walk away with me. Or called Eddie's attention in another direction where he wouldn't see Horkos, or told Horkos to leave his Eris Industries embossed briefcase in his car, or cut Eddie off before he got to the site in the first place, or stood in line in front of Horkos while he got his coffee in the morning with an order so obnoxiously large and complex that he'd have ended up being late for the meeting.

As much as my mind recognized the irrationality of it, I wished I'd done any one of those things. My heart pounded against my ribcage like a battering ram on a castle gate as I strolled through the oscillating light. It's not like doing any of them would have helped the situation—save for the clairvoyance—but I would at least feel better, probably, maybe.

*Dim.*

I wish I'd had access to a time machine. I could have set the dial to this morning and changed Eddie's path, or gone back a month and done a better job of cheering Eddie up at the bar. Gone back and convinced the Edcon corporate guys not to buy those aloos in the first place so things could go back to normal and everyone could be happy again.

If I showed them the consequences of buying the aloos, they'd probably change their plans and keep employing people.

Or maybe they'd just fire Eddie sooner and buy a security aloo as well. I don't know. But if I had a time machine, and I knew what I know now, I'd be able to make a difference. Not that it matters. Time machines are impossible, I think, but the idea comforted me at the time.

I pulled out my phone and texted Marlow.

*Hey babe, you around?*

*Bright.*

A car whizzed by, momentarily awakening the power generating turbines wrapped around the hydro poles from their slumber. Like a championship sprinter running a marathon, they spun swiftly as the starting gun fired before spending all their energy and slowing to a crawl.

The turbines' shadows flickered on the ground, casting the homeless person walking by me in the starring role of their own reel to reel film, buried in so many coats, rags, and shreds of cloth I couldn't see a single bit of human being.

We bumped shoulders and they stumbled about with a grunt before continuing on their zigzagging path. The trail of odour they left behind combined a unique blend of piss, cheap liquor and sewage. How did this person manage to be homeless when everyone seemed to be taken care of through the bottom line or one of the massively overstaffed charities Leopold was talking about?

But maybe this person wasn't actually homeless, just eccentric. Or on the fifth day of a long, self-destructive bender, or they were homeless by choice because they liked to travel and wander. If that's the case why were they buried in jackets in the middle of May?

I always assumed homeless people do that because they don't have anywhere else to put their jacket during the summer, and they don't want to carry around a big heavy bundle of stuff, so it's easier to keep wearing it. Maybe that's nonsense, I don't know.

As they walked away, I ended up fixating on one of the last few remnants of the Toronto Bundschuh Uprising.

During the days before the bottom line, people got pretty desperate. A lot of old buildings burnt to the ground, including a gas station across the street. I guess you can't build on the land where a gas station was, so they left it empty, fenced off and neglected. They didn't get rid of what was left of the store. Instead, they put up one of those heritage commemorative plaques. I stopped to read it.

> On this site on May 1st, 2029, the first act of the Toronto Bundschuh Uprising began. Working class people of all different backgrounds, fearing a future that promised nothing but poverty, began a coordinated general strike across the country to demand government intervention in what they saw as unmitigated corporate greed.
>
> The uprising was spurred by the coordinated kidnapping of the majority of the country's Premiers, including Ontario Premier Martin Wilhelm, who was held in the church that once stood across the street. The standoff with the authorities lasted for several weeks, due largely to support from the local population. Eventually, the Prime Minister agreed to talks, which gradually led to the establishment of the Bottom Line Program. They were inspired by a similar peasant uprising that happened in Germany in the 1700's, from which they got their name.

Wild.

Maybe I should have gone for lunch with Kay and Mateah. That might have been a nice distraction.

Dim.

*BZZT*

*In Sao Paolo babe. Text ya when I get back* ☺

I kept walking.

# 15

The next few weeks were almost normal, though the cloud of Eddie's reaction still hung over the job site, with a broader shadow than any of the skyscrapers around us. We went to work, we went to Black Cat, we went home, we woke up and did it all over again.

Avery, Gael, and Noble joined us most nights at the bar. Keith did the first couple of nights, until he told us he bought an old RV. His plan was to repair it with his wife, and then use it to travel across the continent. That seemed as good a plan as any, though I don't know if I'd enjoy that kind of lifestyle. I never liked travelling when I was younger, and though it's been years since I went anywhere, I doubt that's changed.

New aloos showed up with such frequency at this point that an unboxing was no more notable than a new shipment of material, which arrived, of course, via aloo driven trucks. They'd begun to take care of the HVAC, plumbing, and the electrical. The latter even Mateah admitted they did well. They hadn't bottom lined anybody since the last group, though I'm sure we were due for it, probably to avoid risking another incident.

The maglev ride that morning was even more deserted than usual. My only companion was a blonde teenage girl holding a cage, which contained what I assumed to be her pet. A small furry rodent of some kind. I briefly considered asking her what the thing was and why she was transporting it on the maglev at 6:30 in the morning on a Tuesday, before I realized there was no way for a 38 year old construction worker to talk to a teenage girl he didn't know in an empty maglev car without being intolerably creepy. I didn't need my question answered that badly.

I arrived at work to find an empty job site. The clock on my phone said 6:48. Maybe everyone had slept in.

"Hey, Auden," called Byron. "C'mere a minute, would ya?"

"Oh, uh, hey Byron," I approached him, suppressing that twinge of anxiety one first experiences when called to the principal's office and which never disappears throughout one's adult life when summoned by an authority figure. "What's up?"

"Just wanna check in with ya, see how things are goin'."

"Fine, I guess," I wasn't sure how to respond. Was he fishing for information or something? He'd never checked in on me before.

"Yeah? You're still happy here, are ya?"

"Uh, yeah, yeah everything's fine."

"And you'd tell me if you wasn't happy, yeah?"

I nodded my head.

"Okay then. Just checkin', y'know? There's been lots of changes here I know, and after what happened with Eddie last week some of the crew ain't none too happy about it, at least the few we got left. And head office wants me to talk to all youse, make like everything's good when we got a new change. But I'm glad you're still happy. That's one less guy I gotta worry about."

"Yeah. So what happened to Eddie?"

"I ain't heard nothin'. I tried askin' that Officer Bielak who came by that day, but that guy's dumber'n a can of beans. Couldn't get nothin' out of him. I asked head office too, but they ain't touchin' none of it. They said Eddie wasn't our guy no more and he was trespassin' on company property so they ain't got no responsibility for what happened."

"They didn't even tell you if he's in jail?"

"I don't got the right to know that since I ain't his boss no more." Byron rubbed the back of his neck. "And before you ask, I tried callin' him. No answer."

"So what do we do?"

"I'm workin' on it. Going to see if he's got a court date set up and hopefully get him out on bail. Workin' on head office too. It don't make sense, ya know? If the aloos break down we gotta call youse bottom lined guys back in to work and youse gotta come in. So that seems like Eddie does still work for us, but I ain't a lawyer so I don't know. But for now, we got nothin' to do but get back to work and try to forget about it. But I'll tell ya if someone tells me somethin'."

Great.

"Oh yeah, and here, take this," Byron handed me a plastic orange circle with a key ring attached to it, about the size of a toonie.

"What is it?" I asked.

"After the, uh, incident, head office upgraded the aloos so now they can do security too. When you get to work you gotta show your frog to the first aloo you see, so's they know you're supposed to be here."

"Wait, my what?"

"Your frog, that's what they called it. Weird name I know."

"Are you sure they didn't call it a fob?"

"That don't make no sense, that ain't even a real word."

"Um, okay. Frog it is then. Thanks Byron."

"You got it, just, yeah, like I said, you let me know if you need somethin', ya hear? If I can help, I will."

I made my way to the crane.

I'd hoped my conversation with Byron would have soothed the constant thoughts about what had happened with Eddie, but all he did was pile on more ambiguity. Hour after hour of sitting alone in my crane wasn't exactly conducive to distractions either. Usually that's nice, but it can be disturbing if you're the type of person to get lost in your own thoughts when something negative happens.

So many questions.

Where was Eddie now?

Was he in jail?

What were things like for him in there?

What was he thinking about?

Why did he attack Horkos?

What had he been doing for the last week or so?

Was Horkos okay?

Was Lyla okay?

When is Marlow going to be back?

Why couldn't the aloos recognize me, so I didn't have to carry this frog around?

What would happen if I forgot my frog?

I tried to clear my mind several times, but no matter what I did I couldn't stop thinking about it.

Which made the tinny voice that called up to me that much more surprising.

"HELLO, AUDEN. PLEASE MOVE FIVE BUNDLES OF STEEL I-FRAME BEAMS TO THE 8TH FLOOR CURRENTLY UNDER CONSTRUCTION. THANK YOU."

"Who is this? Is this Hank?" I asked before I realized how stupid a question that was, but the machine answered it anyway.

"I AM AN ERIS INDUSTRIES MODEL EC- TWO ZERO SEVEN THREE COMMUNICATIONS AND LOGISTICS AYY ELL YEW, SERIAL NUMBER THREE NINE ZERO EIGHT AYY DASH FIVE NINE SIX ONE ZERO ZERO THREE SEVEN FOUR ONE ZERO EIGHT. WE HAVE BEEN WORKING TOGETHER SINCE YESTERDAY, AUDEN. DO YOU NOT REMEMBER?"

No, I hadn't.

"Where is Sam?" He had been replaced, of course, and the aloo told me so. Why was I asking such stupid questions today, and why was this thing answering them all? It must have been programmed to answer any question at all from a human, no matter how dumb or obvious.

EC three thousand whatever, I guess they didn't bother giving it a name. The rest of the guys had more of a chance to adjust to the growing aloo presence, but this new aloo was like a punch to the gut. No more chats with Sam. No more updates on what was happening on the ground.

No more connection to the rest of the crew.

Just me alone in my cabin.

Why hadn't anyone told me? Weren't we going to have a going away party for him? Or had it already happened and they hadn't bothered inviting me?

Maybe people weren't in the mood to celebrate much, but I felt like someone should have at least told me something at some point. Without Sam to chat with, would I lose touch with the entire crew? Would I lose touch with reality, spending my days alone in the cabin, talking to no one, my only point of interaction being with a robot?

I made a point right then to start going down every day for lunch.

When lunch time did arrive, I found only two people in the lunch area: Draven (he had the most seniority), and Gill (he was still the cheapest). That's it, just us three. Byron was around too, but he ate in his office.

That must have been why he wanted to talk this morning. To make sure I was alright before I heard the news he'd bottom lined pretty much the entire crew. It's easy to forget about me so high up in the crane, but it would have been nice if somebody filled me in before. Don't know what I would have done differently to prepare for it.

Behind us, our growing squad of aloos continued working. Hank and Blake were the only ones I could see with names painted on their chests; I guess the names were only useful so long as we humans remained the majority. I counted seven within sight, but considering the fact that I couldn't see Clint, there must have been more.

I couldn't believe how quickly the job site had been taken over. It was like I had gone on vacation and come back to find my home completely changed, kind of like the character in my last projection. But I hadn't been on vacation at all, for god's sake. I was still here, every day. I guess I wasn't paying attention.

"Weird weather for this time of year, isn't it?" Draven said to no one in particular.

"Almost...too weird. Almost as if..." he hunched forward in a secretive tone as though he were about to reveal the launch codes for the US nuclear arsenal. "As if it were planned. Can you imagine the power you'd hold if you could control the world's weather?"

"That's impossible though," said Gill.

Big mistake.

Draven didn't believe in the myriad ideas swirling around in his head because of the evidence that supported them. He believed in them because it fulfilled a psychological need. Much like religion, his beliefs were based on faith, not fact.

At least, that's what I remember hearing about conspiracies.

And while we used to have a loudmouth like Eddie or Gael or Brynlee around to shut Draven up, this time it was only Gill and me. Gill, being a young guy trying to start his career, didn't want to make an enemy of anyone who had been there a while. And of course, I never said much to anyone. Neither of us had the good sense to change the subject.

So for the next 20 minutes we were treated to Draven's mind à la carte. Here are a few of the things Gill and I learned:

Now and again Draven would clap me on the arm with "they've infiltrated every level of government" and "it's a portal to hell man! Why do you think they built that big particle collider on the Moon? Think about it!" but for the most part I spent that lunch thinking about how ridiculous Draven's ideas were.

After all, if the reptilians were so advanced that they could travel from another part of the galaxy to ours in search of slaves to do their bidding, you'd think they'd be advanced enough to build their own aloos and wouldn't have to bother with enslaving other species.

We're building all sorts of robots to do our bidding already and we're barely starting to explore our own solar system. And since they're clearly scouring the galaxy to find resources, it seems natural they're running out of their own, because why would you bother travelling all the way across the galaxy if you had enough in your home solar system?

And if that's the case, you'd think fighting a centuries-long battle to gain control of Earth and enslave its inhabitants would make a lot less sense than finding an uninhabited planet and taking those resources. They'd probably run out after the first century or two of trying to gain control of Earth.

And if the Reptilians had the technology to travel from one side of the galaxy to the other, why would they take centuries to enslave us? I wouldn't imagine 18th century muskets would do much against an alien invasion.

"Oh man, that guy is wild," Gill said to me as I walked back toward my crane. "All day, nothing but the wackiest shit. You're going to come down for lunch though still, right? At least there's one other person here who lives on planet Earth."

"Yeah, for sure," I said, while making a point to stay in my crane for lunch. Maybe I could distract myself with a book or a podcast or something. I wasn't supposed to, but there were barely any people left on the job site so I figured I could get away with it. The only person who ever would have noticed is Sam, and something told me EC wasn't going to rat me out.

*This is my life now,* I thought as I sat in the cabin of my crane and flipped through page after page of podcasts, settling on one about the first mission to Mars back in 2028. I would sit in my crane, not talking to anybody, scrolling through to pick a new podcast each day.

Realistically, it wasn't much different than before, but astral projections gave me the idea I was still in control of my days. Rather than passively accepting the entertainment someone else came up with, I made my own.

This is a temporary condition, I told myself. I'd settle for this podcast for now, but somehow I'd force myself to project again.

# 16

Most people, when confronted with their mortality, have only a moment to think about it. A split second glimpse into a truck's grill; a fleeting tussle with a drunk you didn't realize had a knife; an announcement from the pilot to fasten your seat belt.

Not us. We had weeks to sit and contemplate our own demise.

Like a terminally ill friend who keeps fighting even though all rational hope left a long time ago, each of us clung to our plans for when we arrived on the planet. We had even talked about them a few times, but it was blind delusion and we all knew it.

The ship's navigation systems and engine faltered about halfway through our journey. But despite the highly trained engineers on board and expert advice sent from the best minds available back on Earth, the ship remained irreparably damaged.

We were coasting toward a crash landing on Mars, and there was nothing we could do about it.

Using the ship's instruments, I determined we had a 99.38% chance of hitting Mars. If we did, we would do it at 3:42 am GMT, on March 8th, 2070, give or take an hour. Good news, I guess. If we were off course and shot out into space, we'd be dead for sure. But if we somehow survived a crash landing on Mars, we could set up a distress signal and Earth would know where to send help.

Even better, we might even crash near our destination, New Jamestown. The old NASA base they built back in the 2030's had been abandoned a few months in after their funding was cut, but the station's systems were all monitored from Earth. As far as we could tell, it was still in working condition and could support human life.

Everything looked good. Or at least, as good as could be expected given the circumstances. We made a minor course correction which set our approach to Mars at an angle that would allow us to skid along the surface before coming to a stop. The impact would still be heavy, but not quite as bad as it could be. Sort of like jumping off the top of a skyscraper and doing a somersault as you land on the ground to distribute the force of the impact.

We helped each other into our EVA suits and gathered in the rear of the ship. It was a storage area which doubled as a safety room in case of a crash, and given the circumstances it was the safest place any of us could have been. Each of us had our own spot in the room, complete with a harness surrounded by human-shaped, marshmallowy padding.

Two empty spots sat directly across from me, which belonged to Emma and Amelia, the ship's pilots, who were in the cockpit doing their best to control our descent with the systems that remained. We strapped each other in and hoped.

We clung desperately to hope. We dug our nails into hope so intensely our fingers bled. We bit down on hope so hard our teeth shattered and our jaws broke. We squeezed hope so tightly that our shoulders dislocated and our ribs shattered and our lungs collapsed. There was no other option. The only thing that could tear us from that hope was death itself.

Well, that, and the meteor that hit us.

I say meteor, but I have no idea what it actually was. There's a small amount of human made debris floating around Mars from the shattered satellites and other failed exploratory missions, but it's nowhere near the amount orbiting Earth. It could have been that, or one of the millions of rocks in orbit, leftover ingredients from the formation of our solar system. The ship's hull was reinforced against impacts from space debris up to 10 centimetres thick, at a velocity of up to 1500 kilometres per hour.

Imagine a grapefruit travelling about twice the speed of a bullet.

But instead of a grapefruit, something a lot harder hit us, like a rock or a chunk of metal. Definitely not a grapefruit, since as far as I know there are no grapefruit trees anywhere near Mars, and I didn't see any juice splattered about the rest of the ship. But anyway, it was something bigger than a grapefruit, and hard enough to pierce through our hull.

NASA had monitored all the Mars orbit objects they could find and plotted a course that should have steered us clear, and the ratio of objects large enough to damage us to empty space for us to safely travel must have been somewhere around one hundred quadrillion to one.

Whatever it was, it tore clean through the bow. Like the hands of a clock on the end of a drill, we whipped around and around as we came closer and closer to Mars. All around me my fellow crew members vomited and lost consciousness.

The last thing I remember was wishing I'd bought a lottery ticket before I left.

I awoke to a grey-green lightning bolt across my vision, flickering in and out. No, not a lightning bolt. The flicker was from an electrical fire.

The bolt was a crack across the glass in my helmet.

The grey-green was vomit.

The pain was unbelievable.

I took a deep breath and felt a sharp pain stab through my chest. I winced, feeling the vomit stuck to my cheeks cracking and flaking off as I did. Probably a broken rib. I could manage okay, so long as I took shorter breaths.

It smelled awful.

My left arm hurt, but it wasn't broken.

My head hurt.

Everything hurt.

I checked my suit's internal monitoring system. Other than the visor crack, which was slowly leaking air, my suit was in working order. There was a fire, so the room hadn't depressurized at least.

I reached for my helmet, only to be reminded of the straps that held me in place. My lifelines. I had to cut them loose.

It was harder than I expected. Every push forward with my emergency knife, every pull back, caused a stabbing pain in my chest, which got worse the longer I struggled.

Once I cut the last strap loose, I wiggled free of the padding, and fell flat on my face.

Oh yeah, gravity.

In space, you take a lot of terrestrial things for granted. You become accustomed to floating from place to place. The pressure of gravity pulling down on your body, the idea of your body having any weight at all, becomes an alien concept. Your muscles atrophy in a way that even hours each day on a treadmill or an exercise bike can't stave off.

My helmet smacked against the floor, deepening the lightning bolt across my vision.

I laid face down on the floor of a broken ship 225 million kilometres away from home. It hurt to move. It hurt to breathe.

Just stay here for a while.

Just rest, close your eyes. You can deal with this later.

No, I thought, shaking my head and wincing at the throbbing pain. The fire.

The fire hadn't grown, but nor had it shrunk. Smouldering out from one of the electrical ducts that ran under the square floor tiles, most of which had broken loose, it was swallowing up my precious imported lifeblood.

Only one of us could survive this.

I turned my helmet lamp on and took a better look around. There were floor tiles everywhere, in various states of destruction. Some had lodged themselves deeply in the padding on the walls, which easily gave way to a four cornered projectile.

And one had lodged itself firmly in the chest of Lieutenant John Kragar, the ship's chief engineer.

The tile was almost perfectly horizontal, a connect the dots between the COSMEX emblem on the right side of his chest, and the Australian flag emblazoned on the left. It would have sliced both of his lungs, his vagus nerve, and probably his heart and spine clean in two.

There was no way he was anything but dead.

I cut John's body loose and pulled it from its cradle. He fell into my arms, setting off an explosion of pain in my chest that knocked us both to the floor in a crumpled heap.

Even with Mars' reduced gravity, and my damaged rib cage screaming at me to relieve the pressure, it took several minutes to rally my impotent muscles to push him off me.

Pulling myself to my hands and knees once again, I grabbed John's body by the hand and dragged it over to the fire. His spacesuit smouldered for a moment as the fire fizzled out.

Thanks, John. I removed my helmet and took a deep breath. The stale, recycled air I had been breathing for the last year smelled wonderful, comforting, and downright pleasant when compared with the vomitorium my head was just in.

Using the helmet as a mirror, I took my first look at myself as a new Martian immigrant. Dark swamps pooled below my eyes, a morass of sweat, tears, exhaustion, and half digested rations. I wiped as much of it away as I could, but it didn't make much of a difference.

Deep breath. Keep going.

The rest of John's suit was useless, but his helmet was pristine. Since he wouldn't be using it any time soon, I removed the bolts on his helmet and set it aside.

Thanks again, John.

Returning to Earth was impossible, at least for now. My best hope would be to make my way to New Jamestown and stay there until Earth could send help.

What if we were on the other side of the planet? It could take months to walk all the way there, and even if we did have enough supplies to make the journey, I could barely walk across the room, let alone march the Martian landscape.

What if New Jamestown was damaged? Maybe the life support system wouldn't start up again. What if the communication system is damaged and I can't contact Earth? What if it does work but Earth can't send help and I'm stuck here on Mars all alone forever? A hundred thousand things could go wrong, and if they did I'd be dead.

Deep breath. Keep going.

I had to proceed on the assumption that it was still working and I could reach and access it. Otherwise, I may as well walk outside and take off my helmet. I got up to check my fellow crew members. None, save for John, were visibly harmed. Maybe I would have a companion to help me through this ordeal. Maybe we'd return to Earth one day and sit on the porch together, two old farts recounting the story of that crazy journey we went on to Mars and back.

But no. One by one I confirmed their deaths. One by one my hope dwindled until it was clear I was alone.

The cargo bay had a heavy loader aloo and two Martian roving vehicles. If any of them had survived the crash, it would make things much easier. But I'd have to get there first.

Opening the seal on the door was a risk in itself. The corridor could have a leak in it.

I crawled to John's helmet and lifted it to my head. Another explosion of pain in my chest shook me to the ground. Collecting myself, I sealed the helmet into place, and dragged myself to my feet.

The first time I'd ever stood on Mars.

I pushed the lever forward to open the seal on the door, then pulled it toward me. No change in pressure, good. I staggered into the corridor and pulled the lever to seal the first door behind me, the heaviest lever anyone ever pulled. Peering through the porthole on the next door, I saw the long hallway leading to our sleeping quarters. No visible damage, other than the lack of light.

A few hours ago, we'd used the corridor's railings to pull ourselves along in zero gravity. Now I used them to prop up my flimsy muscles. I struggled down the corridor to my quarters and checked my computer terminal. It was dead, of course. So were the terminals in everyone else's quarters. But the ship's interior itself, somehow, was mostly in good shape.

Hope swelled as I began to imagine the rest of the ship may have been too. The meteor blasted a hole in the hull, sure, but maybe the rest of it was in decent condition. Maybe I could repair the hole and get it spaceworthy again.

I took a look through the next porthole to see the mess. It was, well, a mess. A prison riot or grade school food fight couldn't have caused such chaos. Memories of the meals I had shared with my friends flooded into my mind.

Amelia's obsession with history, Finn's boisterous attitude, Emma's inquisitive nature, the LA Dodgers baseball cap John always wore, the many games of zero gravity food catch we used to play.

But now they were gone. I was all alone.

Maybe not. Emma and Amelia were in the cockpit during the crash. There was a possibility the two of them had survived. A slim possibility, but I had to check anyway.

The next section was the cargo hold. I looked through the porthole again and was greeted by a sea of black and a star speckled sky. Most of the cargo hold, and the entire front half of the ship, was gone.

The one light that hadn't been shattered illuminated a small patch of the Martian soil about a metre below the broken edge of the ship. Anything more than a few metres away was utter darkness.. Fortunately, Mars has the same constellations Earth does. Using the constellation Cygnus, the closest thing Mars has to a North Star, I discovered I was facing northeast.

The rovers were gone, but the loader towered patiently in its restraints. Its square body was at least four metres tall and two wide. Painted with a reflective bright green to stand out against the Martian landscape, which it was designed to travel using a pair of caterpillar tracks. One of its four arms was damaged, but it looked more or less okay.

Fortunately, the loader responded to voice commands. A deep voice bellowed through the comm system in my helmet.

"UNIT E-R-H-N-K THREE FOUR ONE FOUR ONE ONE EIGHT DASH THREE EIGHT TWO SEVEN REPORTING FOR DUTY. ANALYZING COORDINATES... COORDINATES CONFIRMED. ONE ZERO DECIMAL THREE TWO DEGREES NORTH LATITUDE, ONE ZERO FOUR DECIMAL SIX SEVEN DEGREES EAST LONGITUDE ON THE PLANET MARS. BEGINNING SYSTEM DIAGNOSTICS. ESTIMATED COMPLETION TIME: THREE HOURS, TWENTY THREE MINUTES."

If the loader was correct, we'd crashed in the middle of Amazonis, a relatively flat area north of Olympus Mons.

New Jamestown was about 3000 km away. The trip would take me two full months on foot, and there's no way I could bring enough supplies with me to survive the trip even if my muscles didn't feel like they'd been replaced with rubber bands.

But the loader could move up to 25 kilometres per hour. No Ferrari, but it could ferry me, and a lot of supplies, to New Jamestown in just a couple of weeks. Even better, it could travel day and night with only a few hours of rest to recharge its solar batteries.

If it worked.

I'd find out in three hours, twenty three minutes.

I used the time to search through the ship. Loaded as many bags as I could with packs of food paste, water, spare oxygen tanks, a tool kit, a food printer, a tool printer, first aid kits, computers, anything that still worked. I searched my fellow crew members one last time, confirming their deaths before taking their oxygen tanks.

In all, I managed to gather about sixteen days worth of oxygen. I could stretch it out to twenty in a pinch.

A lot could go wrong.

"DIAGNOSTIC COMPLETE," the loader broadcast to me and nine corpses. "SOLAR POWER OPERATING AT SIXTY TWO PERCENT CAPACITY. LOCOMOTION OPERATING AT EIGHTY EIGHT PERCENT CAPACITY. RIGHT UPPER ARM OPERATING AT NINETY THREE PERCENT CAPACITY. LEFT UPPER ARM OPERATING AT THIRTEEN PERCENT CAPACITY..."

On it went with its diagnostic report, but I stopped listening. It could move and it could charge itself—the first piece of real good news I'd had on Mars. After loading it with my supplies, I undid its restraints and it rolled itself out onto the Martian surface. Then I struggled onto its back, trying to ignore the pain in my chest. Using a parachute, I tied a makeshift hammock to its back, my home for the next 3000 kilometres.

"Loader, this is Lieutenant Auden Black." I spoke into my suit's comm system.

"ACKNOWLEDGED, LIEUTENANT. WHAT ARE YOUR ORDERS?"

"Locate the foresection of the ship."

"THE SHIP'S FORESECTION IS LOCATED AT NINE DECIMAL THREE TWO DEGREES NORTH LATITUDE, NINE ZERO DECIMAL FOUR ZERO DEGREES EAST LONGITUDE."

Several hundred kilometres away.

In the exact opposite direction of New Jamestown.

Even if Amelia and Emma had survived, it would take me days to get to them, if the loader lasted that long. And I barely had enough oxygen and water for one person, let alone three.

"Loader, locate the rovers."

"UNABLE TO COMPLY. ROVER TRANSPONDERS HAVE BEEN DAMAGED OR DEACTIVATED."

So much for that idea. "Loader, travel to 14.5 degrees south latitude, 175.4 degrees east longitude."

"*BUZZ* ERROR. IT IS RECOMMENDED TO USE A MARTIAN ROVING VEHICLE. E-R-H-N-K UNITS ARE NOT RECOMMENDED FOR JOURNEYS OF MORE THAN FIVE KILOMETRES. PLEASE CONFIRM ORDER."

"I wasn't designed for long journeys either, but here we are. Order confirmed. Let's go."

"ACKNOWLEGED."

The first few metres of movement brought a wave of relief over me. The ship was destroyed and my friends were dead, but I was going to survive.

I looked back at the remains of my ship as it shrunk in the distance. The loader's body absorbed most of the shocks, turning them into soft vibrations before they reached the amniotic cocoon in which I lay, rocking me gently to sleep.

The Sun rose to the east, a pale pinprick less than half the size of what you'd see on Earth. It cast thousands of long shadows across each rock on the surface, a forest of darkness punctuated with the occasional red spatter.

Billions of people back on Earth were looking up at the same star, enjoying its warmth. Thinking about that made me feel less alone. I imagined my family and friends back home.

Imagine their reaction when I reach New Jamestown and let them know I'm alive. You thought I was dead, you even had a funeral for me, you suckers! I regret to inform you that you wasted your time and money and tears and heartache.

Oh, yeah everyone else is still dead though, sorry to get anyone else's hopes up. But hey, send me a video of the funeral, yeah? I want to hear my eulogy. I hope NASA didn't cheap out and serve cold cuts on crummy white bread. They sent us to die on Mars—the least they could do was get some nice rye bread, or pumpernickel or something.

God, I missed eating real food.

Behind me jutted Olympus Mons, the largest mountain in the solar system. It was the only remarkable feature in the sea of monotony. I took the opportunity to snap a few photos using the camera on my suit. At least this mission will provide humanity with something of value.

Gratitude swelled within me as I recognized I was the first person to look at it directly, a feeling that distracted me enough from the pain as I drifted off to sleep.

My heavy heartbeat woke me up, like an unwelcome house guest knocking at the door. As I opened my eyes, motion at the edge of my vision seized my attention and fear gripped my heart. When I turned my head to see what it was, the movement disappeared.

What could it be? There isn't supposed to be anything else alive on this planet. Nothing from Earth, anyway. But everything we know about Mars is that it's completely lifeless.

It must be the oxygen deprivation. I switched the oxygen pack, which gave me three days of air at the current rate of flow.

"Loader, scan for nearby life forms."

"I DETECT NO LIFE FORMS WITHIN FIFTY KILOMETRES OF OUR LOCATION. SHOULD I EXTEND MY SCAN?"

"No, that's fine. Confirm our coordinates"

"WE ARE LOCATED AT ONE THREE DECIMAL THREE DEGREES NORTH LATITUDE, ONE FIVE TWO DECIMAL ONE DEGREES EAST LATITUDE."

I looked behind us and saw nothing but the loader's tracks and the horizon, as flat as the one before me. Motion tickled the edges of my vision again as I drifted back into a restless sleep.

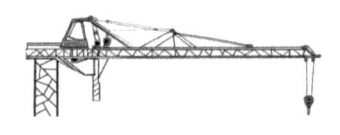

Awake.

So itchy but I can't scratch.

Damn this suit.

This suit?

Where am I? The ship?

No, Mars.

Right. The ship crashed.

Am I at New Jamestown?

No not yet.

So why am I not moving?

Why am I lying on the ground in the middle of the Martian wastes?

The hammock on the ground under me torn on the sides.

The bags on the ground ahead of me.

The tracks stretching in both directions as far as I can see.

I must have fallen off as I slept.

"Loader."

Static.

"Loader do you copy?"

Static.

"Loader this is Lieutenant Auden Black, please respond."

Static.

I checked my coordinates. Still another 800 kilometres to New Jamestown.

Only a day of oxygen left in my tank.

I checked the bags nearby and found about a week's worth of oxygen.

Still not enough to walk 800 kilometres.

No food or water left in my suit.

Weak, rubbery muscles.

But I had to try.

My heart pounded heavily against my chest, out of fear as much as oxygen deprivation. My lungs forced me to breathe deeply even as my chest screamed in protest. Every step was torture, every moment a new nightmare, but I walked on.

My vision narrowed.

No, I had to stay conscious.

My throat hurt, my tongue stuck to the sides of my mouth.

Cold. So cold.

So much pain.

      Movement.

*What was that?*

"No. No get away from me!"

*Step.*

*Walk.*

*Keep walking.*

*Don't stop.*

*Keep walking.*

*Thirsty.*

*Tired.*

*Can't stop.*

*Afraid.*

*Can't stop.*

*Nothingness.*

*Can't stop.*

*"This can't be the end."*

*Air. Need air. New oxygen pack.*

*Deep breath. Pain*

*Can't stop.*

*Alone.*

*I'm going to die alone.*

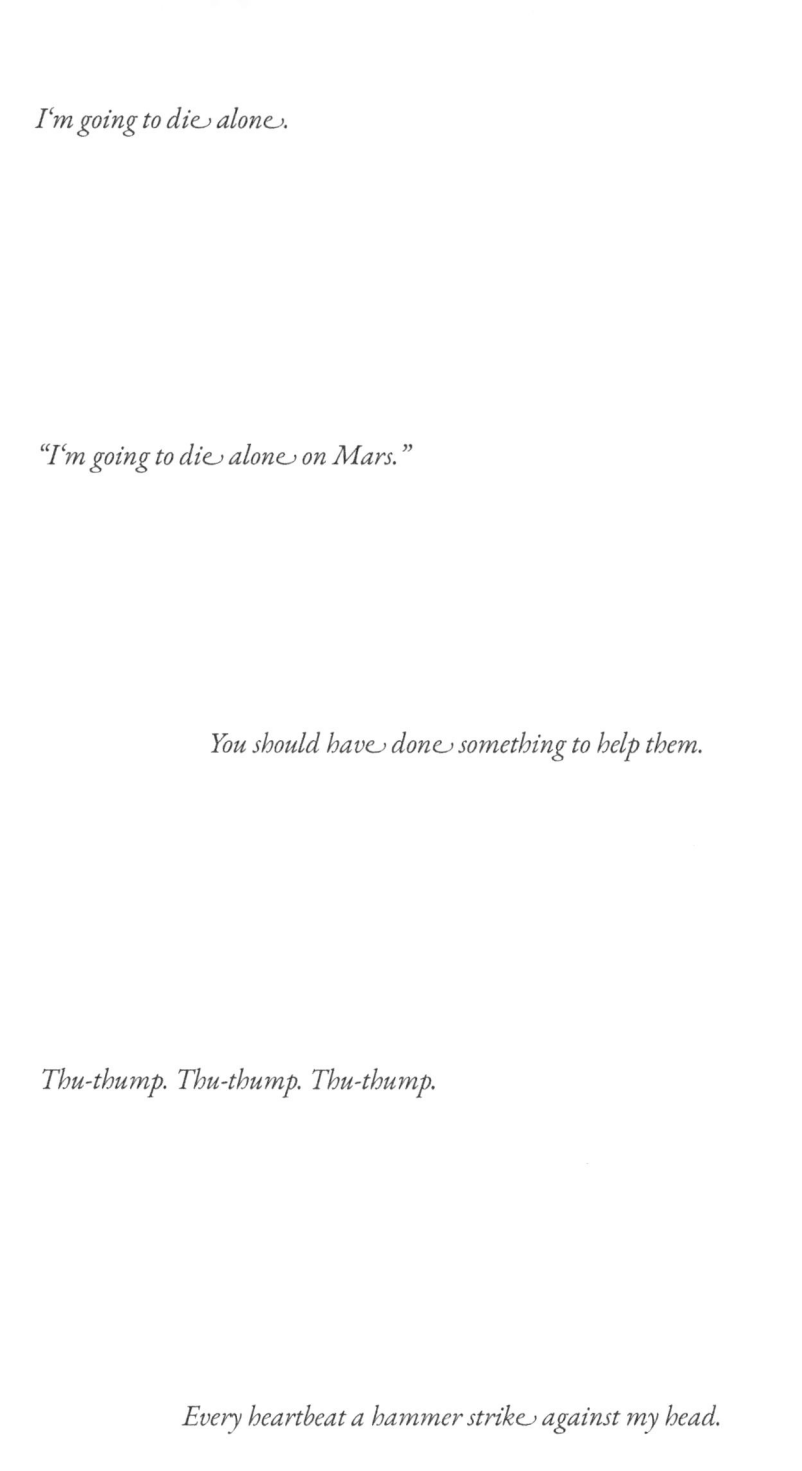

*"I'm going to die alone on Mars."*

*You should have done something to help them.*

*Thu-thump. Thu-thump. Thu-thump.*

*Every heartbeat a hammer strike against my head.*

*Can't stop.*

*Help. Help me.*

*"Loader, come in."*
*Static.*

*Bugs*
*crawling on*
*my skin.*

*Can't stop.*




















*"Auden?"*

















*Is someone calling me?*

*Is someone there?*

"Auden, are you there?"

I'm here.

Who are you?

"Earth to Auden."

*Earth?*

*Please save me.*

*Please.*

Please.

# 17

Beep. Beep. Beep. Beep.

"GOOD MORNING, MX. BLACK. IT IS GOOD TO SEE YOU AWAKE."

The robotic voice, so bright, so singsong, so pleasant. Was that the loader? It didn't sound like the loader.

Beep. Beep. Beep. Beep.

"HNK? Is that you?"

"I AM NOT AN ERIS INDUSTRIES HNK SERIES. I AM AN AUTOMED RX THREE TWO EIGHT SERIES ALOO, BUT YOU CAN CALL ME NURSE."

A nurse aloo? Did they leave a nurse aloo behind in New Jamestown?

Was I in New Jamestown?

A sliver of bright light stabbed through my eyelids as I opened them. It felt like I hadn't used them in weeks.

Beep. Beep. Beep. Beep.

"How did you get to Mars?"

"I DO NOT UNDERSTAND, MX. BLACK. THIS IS MT. SINAI HOSPITAL IN TORONTO. WE ARE ON EARTH, NOT MARS."

"How did I get here?"

"YOU WERE BROUGHT HERE BY YOUR EMPLOYER, MR. BYRON HOLMSTEAD. HE FOUND YOU IN A STATE OF DELERIUM WHILE YOU WERE OPERATING YOUR CRANE."

Byron?

Crane?

Shit.

"How long have I been here?"

"TODAY IS FRIDAY, JULY TWENTY-FIFTH, 2053. YOU ARRIVED HERE FOUR DAYS AGO. YOU HAVE BEEN IN A COMA SINCE YOU ARRIVED."

"What? How?"

"SEVERE DEHYDRATION AND KIDNEY FAILURE."

I needed some better answers than this aloo could give me.

"Can you contact Byron?"

"MR. HOLMSTEAD HAS BEEN REGULARLY UPDATED ON YOUR STATUS, AS HAVE YOUR IMMEDIATE FAMILY AND NEXT OF KIN. I WILL CONTACT MR. HOLMSTEAD NOW."

As I wondered whether I even had a next of kin, the display screen on the aloo's chest became a teleconference window and dialed Byron's number.

"Hello? Oh, Auden, you're awake. Y'alright?"

"I feel awful. What am I doing here?"

"I'll come up and see ya in a few minutes. I'm actually here at the hospital right now with Avery. Poor guy drank too much and made himself sick, but the doctor said he's going to be okay. Hey Avery, you wanna say hi to Auden?"

He shoved the camera in Avery's face, who was lying in a hospital bed looking about as terrible as I felt.

"Oh, hey Auden," Avery said weakly.

"Uh, hey Avery. How are you?" *Stupid question. He's in the hospital with alcohol poisoning you idiot, how do you think he is?*

"I've been better. I guess we're neighbours for now, huh?"

"I'll come up and see you in a few minutes Auden. Is that alright, nurse?"

"MX. BLACK MAY ENTERTAIN VISITORS."

"Okay, see you in a bit."

The screen went black for a moment before lighting up again.

"YOUR NEXT OF KIN IS ATTEMPTING TO CONTACT YOU. DO YOU WISH TO TAKE THE CALL?"

I filled my lungs with the stale hospital air. "Okay nurse, connect the call."

"YES, MX. BLACK."

"Auden, my sweet, sweet darling, how are you?" my mother's voice piped through the nurse's speaker as her face appeared on its view screen.

"Hi mom." The spaces between the EKG beeps grew smaller. "The nurse says I'll be okay."

"Oh good, good honey. I was telling my friend Sarah about what happened and she told me about when she was a kid and went to a party and took too much molly and woke up in a hospital, is that what you did?"

"No, mom."

"Because you can tell me about it honey, I won't get mad. Even though you probably shouldn't do drugs at work, but that's okay, I'm not going to judge. It reminded me of when I was younger and had so much fun partying, Sarah and I were inseparable. The toxic twins they used to call us, did I ever tell you that?"

"Yes, mom."

"But if you are doing drugs, you know you can talk to me, right? I work with people with addictions all day, so if you have a drug problem, I can help you, honey. Do you have a drug problem?"

"No mom, I'm not doing drugs."

"Okay good, I'm glad to hear that. Because I know how much fun they can be at first, but I also know how destructive they can be later on, and I hope you aren't..."

*It always comes back to drugs. Why does she always think I'm on drugs? I've never tried anything harder than pot.*

*Do I look like an addict or something?*

I sat up a bit to look in the mirror across the room.

"...her parents' money, and that..."

*Okay, fair. I don't look great right now.*

"...boss said you were bottom lined too, that's great honey. Your..."

*But I'm in the hospital, how good could you expect someone to look?*

"...travel and have fun with your friends..."

*I'm sure I'll look better once I rehydrate.*

"...didn't know what to do with our lives..."

I took a sip of the cocktail of nutrients on the table beside my bed. It tasted a little like baking soda, or what I imagine baking soda would taste like.

"...what are you going to do next?"

"Uh, I don't know" I stumbled.

"Call some of your little friends from work and see what they're doing, that's a good start. Anyway I have to go, but I'm glad you're feeling better honey, take care, love you!"

*click*

*Beep. Beep. Beep. Beep.*

*sigh*

She did have one point, though.

I decided to give Sam a call.

"Auden, hey!" Sam said as his head appeared where my mother had been a moment ago. "Where are you? Are you still in the hospital? Are you alright?"

"Hey, Sam. Yeah, I'm okay. I don't know what happened," I lied. "One minute I was up in the crane and the next I was in a hospital bed. I think I just lost track of time."

"Lost track of time? Byron told me what happened. You were up there for three days!"

"Four, actually. Yeah, it's weird. I don't know what happened," I repeated.

"Come on Auden. In all the years I've known you, this has never happened before. Are you sure you don't know what happened?"

"Well." The ECG machine beeped faster. "I always daydreamed when I was up in the crane. That's why I was always a little weird when you first called up to me. It's the only thing that kept me sane up there. But when you checked in on me it helped keep me grounded. Without that I guess I just lost track of time."

"Yeah, I know man. You're up there by yourself all day; of course you had to do something to pass the time. No one loves cranes so much that they can't wait to get in them. So what were you thinking about up there?"

"Oh, I don't know, heh. All sorts of stuff. Depends on the day." That's about all I wanted to explain. "Anyway, how are you now that you're bottom lined?"

"Nice segue. As soon as Byron told me, I booked plane tickets to Kenya for my family. It's only been a few days, but we love it here. Hey girls, come say hi to my friend Auden!" Sam pulled the camera far enough away to cram three women into the lens with him, revealing his upper body, which, shockingly, was covered not by a white t-shirt and overall straps, but a bright red dashiki with a yellow and gold pattern across his shoulders. "Auden, this is Vivienne, and this is Londyn, and this is my wife Delia."

"Hi Auden! Did you work with my daddy?" asked Londyn, the younger looking one.

"Yeah, I did. Your dad and I worked together for a long time."

"That's true Auden, I think we were on that crew together for what, 15 years?"

"Something like that, yeah. I started with Byron's crew right out of school. Did you bring Lucy with you?"

"No, there aren't many good highways to drive here so we left her at home. But we've booked a trip to Korea next year, and Lucy will definitely be coming with us then. So what are you going to do now that you've been bottom lined?"

"I'm not sure. I hadn't given it much thought."

"What do you mean you haven't given it much thought? You just told me all you did up in the crane was think."

"Yeah..." I shrugged. I didn't have an answer. "Have you talked to any of the other guys?"

"Yeah, a couple. You should give them a shout too. Noble was asking about you, actually. I'm sure he'd be glad to hear from you. Anyway, we need to get going. Our first Swahili lesson starts soon. Kwaheri! That's 'goodbye' in Swahili."

"Kwaheri Sam. Kwaheri, everyone."

The screen faded out in a chorus of kwaheris and waving hands.

Noble? Why was Noble asking about me? I barely knew the guy.

Before I had a chance to find out, Byron entered the room.

"Auden, hey buddy, how ya feelin'?"

"I've been better. What happened anyway?"

"You were sayin' some strange stuff on the radio. Somethin' about dyin' on Mars. I called up to you a few times but you didn't say nothin' that made no sense to me so I climbed up to your crane there and found you all delirious like. Do you remember?"

"I remember being up in the crane, talking with that new aloo, what's it called? FG two five something?"

"EC-2073. I just call it Ee-See."

"Ee-See, sure. I was talking to Ee-See, and then I was here. I don't know what happened," I lied.

"What did the nurse say?"

"Not much, actually. Nurse, what's my prognosis?"

"YOU SUFFERED FROM SEVERE DEHYDRATION AND SLEEP DEPRIVATION, HOWEVER YOUR BRAIN SHOWS NO SIGN OF PERMANENT DAMAGE. THE DOCTOR WILL BE IN TO SEE YOU SHORTLY AND WILL GIVE YOU A MORE DETAILED ANALYSIS."

"I looked at the sign in sheet. It said you were there for four days straight, from Thursday mornin' 'til Monday mornin' when I found ya. That was a mistake, right? You just forgot to sign out?"

"I guess so."

"Okay good, 'cause HR's been askin' about what happened. If they call ya, make sure ya tell 'em that, eh?"

"Okay."

Enough of this. "I just talked to Sam. He seems to be happy in Kenya. How are the other guys?"

"Hang on, just wanna make it clear—what are ya gonna tell 'em?"

"I forgot to sign out."

"Okay good, s'important stuff, huh? For the, uh, paperwork, y'know? Just gotta make everyone's job easier, you'd have to fill out a bunch of it too, so this is good for you too, yeah? Really, it's more help for you than anyone else, okay?"

"Okay."

"Okay." Byron nodded.

"Okay..."

"Okay, so uhh...well you saw Avery. He messed himself up real good. Guy said he drank two bottles of wine and a dozen shots of vodka in one sitting, the maniac. I think he's going to be okay though. Wasn't an accident on the job or nothin'. Draven bought a cabin and moved up north with his family, which shouldn't be surprising to no one. Mateah and Kay started a business making LifeSim games, which I guess ain't a surprise neither. Gill's traveling; last I heard, he was in Hong Kong visiting some family there. Keith is traveling too; he bought one of them RVs and took off around the country with his wife. Haven't heard nothin' from none of the other guys."

"Nothing about Eddie?"

"Last I heard, he was out on bail. That was a few days ago though. He don't answer my calls no more." He trailed off for a moment. "Anyway, I'm glad you're alright. We got a new aloo to operate the crane, so you take as much time as you need to get better."

"I'm bottom lined?"

"Yeah, the whole crew is now. Head office said they're working on a way to connect all the aloos together so you can feed 'em a schematic and they know what to build from top to bottom. But that ain't ready yet, so for now it's me and all them damn robots. Maybe I'll get to join the rest of you lazy bums someday too. They're even bottom lining each other, head office sent an attachment for the HNKs so's they can do the backhoe work, so we sent the backhoe aloo back. So I guess I'm last in line, even behind the robots. Anyway, I gotta get back to the job site. Those aloos gotta be babysat, and I got some paperwork to fill out about this whole thing. One of these days you gotta teach me how you stayed sane all those years workin' by yerself up in that crane. I'm going to need some tips. Take care of yourself, Auden. I'll check up on ya again later. And if the workplace safety guys call, don't answer, alright? The company's gonna handle all that for ya, don't worry about it."

"Thanks Byron. By the way, Sam said Noble was asking about me. Any idea what that's about?"

"No idea. Give him a ring, I guess," Byron said as he left.

I guess.

I asked the nurse aloo to contact Noble. After a moment, three bright, vivid colours appeared on the screen. It took me a moment to recognize the peach as the sky, the baby blue as an ocean, and the deep fuchsia as a beach. A few splotches of neon green floated on the water, giving off an organic looking light.

On the beach, a few logs and half-eaten trees were home to a few dozen small lizards sitting on a branch and scurried about. Other than that, nothing. I mean, yes it was pretty, but I wasn't looking for pretty. I was looking for Noble. For a long moment, nothing happened except for me wondering whether the nurse had made a mistake and turned on a movie or something. And that's when a voice spoke.

"Who approaches come forth," it replied. Each word sounded like it was being inhaled through a gravel filled popcorn popper.

"Um, hello?" I said.

"Who approaches come forth," the voice repeated.

One of the lizards then stood up on its hind legs as the screen zoomed in on it. Horizontal black slits slashed through its green eyes, surrounded by the scaly grey ridges of its damp skin. Its spade-shaped head culminated in two tiny nostrils and a thin mouth, devoid of lips or teeth. It wore a long blue jacket that extended down its thighs, open at the front with two sets of buttons on either side of its white breast, white pants with black boots rising up past its knees, and a tall cylindrical cap on its head.

If I didn't know any better, I'd say Napoleon had begun hiring lizards to command his army.

Then again, I wasn't even really sure I knew any better. I was suffering from severe dehydration, after all.

"Umm, I think I have the wrong number."

"No," the creature replied. "You I know Auden, your friend Noble I once was."

"...huh?"

"On Kurtadam I live on the shores of the Krozagrumg Ocean among my people and traders, I am known as Merketorix, I serve my people by catching food and bringing it to village to trade."

I paused for a moment, taking it all in. Noble, Merketorix, whatever—the thing's face stood motionless. "So, uh, you're Noble then?"

"Yes, Auden, the being once known as Noble contacted the humans he once worked alongside to join him in uniting their spirits with that of the realm of Vast."

The lizard—Noble—Merketorix, I guess—shot out his tongue, snapping a large flying insect out of the air and into his mouth in the blink of an eye. Its translucent, veined wings hung out of the lizard's mouth for the first few bites as it twisted and turned in digital agony.

"I...uh..." There were so many questions in my head I didn't know where to start.

"To speak in human terms, I invite you to join myself and Adikaros the being once known as Karter in the LifeSim program Vast, where all live in peace and tranquility along the shores of the Krozagrumg."

"Did you say Karter is there too?"

"Adikaros."

"I'm still confused. Can I talk to Kart—I mean, Adikaros?"

"I will summon."

We waited a moment while the software connected with Karter, Adikara, whatever. Merketorix's face jerked about every few seconds or so, remaining completely motionless in between.

The window on the nurse's chest split in two. Merketorix moved to the right side, and another being appeared on the left, a face more feline than reptilian, yet unmistakably bipedal

"Oh, hey Merketorix. You aren't due to deliver your remzelks for another three cycles. What's up?"

"Auden."

"Oh, Auden, how are you? It's been ages! You must come visit us on Kurtadam, it's so beautiful here!"

"Um, Adikaros, is it? I'm confused. What happened to you both?"

"Oh, we look a little different than the last time we saw you, don't we? After I was bottom lined, I contacted Merketorix here to try out his LifeSim program. And it's been life changing."

"But you're a cat."

"Well when I got my own LifeSim I got to choose whatever body I wanted. Instead of replacing my robot legs with human looking ones, I changed my body to fit them. Running across the open plains just south of Krozagrumg as fast as I can... There's really nothing like it. You should try it, Auden. Actually, Kay and Mateah built a great world just a few parsecs away, with these delicious golden rivers that taste like watermelons and trees that grow fresh pickles. Merketorix and I are saving up for a flight to go visit. He just needs to keep delivering me those high quality remzelks. We should have enough in a week or so, but we can wait for you if you want to come with us."

"Yeah maybe. I, uh, have to go, but I'll uh, call you later okay?"

"Sure, call me anytime. Take care!"

"Goodbye."

The screen went black.

Gael was right. Noble lives in a frog simulator.

And Kay and Mateah build frog simulators.

And Karter is a cat?

Well, at least they found something to do.

And I guess I can't judge—in my mind, I went to just as many strange places, though I was always a human at least. But does that really make a difference? Are you less of a weirdo if you spend all day in a fantasy world but you stay human?

Either way, I decided staying in the real world for awhile was best for my health. No LifeSim for me, and no projecting either. But they did seem happy, I guess. And Sam is obviously happy too. I guess Keith and Gill are, and Draven is at least away from the global worldwide new world order conspiracy or whatever, so he must be happy.

And if things worked out for them, maybe the bottom line isn't so bad. Maybe things worked out for the other guys too. Maybe things worked out okay for Gael, Brynlee, Leopold, and the rest of them. Maybe things even worked out okay for Eddie.

Yeah, things for Eddie must have turned out okay. Of course, things have worked out okay for Eddie. They worked out okay for everyone else, why not him too? Okay sure, Avery went through a rough patch, but he'll be alright. So Eddie must be doing alright too.

Better than alright, he must be doing great. He must have gotten a court date and talked to a judge, and his lawyer would have told the judge Eddie had a drinking problem and was having a tough time with his recent bottom lining. The judge would have been sympathetic and sentenced him to anger management and community service. Maybe Mr. Horkos would have dropped the charges once he saw that Eddie was getting help, and Eddie would have started seeing a therapist for what he had gone through. He'd sit down in a nice, brightly lit office with a comfortable couch in one corner and a nice tall fern in the other and the therapist would suggest Eddie meet with Mr. Horkos and apologize for the harm he had caused, and he'd do it, and Horkos would accept his apology, and they'd embrace in a brotherly hug and maybe even become friends.

Yeah, things must have worked out for Eddie.

I'll give him a call and see how well he's doing.

I can't wait to see how well he's doing.

"Nurse, contact Eddie Hallstrom please," I said, as much with pride as with excitement.

"RIGHT AWAY MX. BLACK."

The phone rang once.

Twice.

"WITH GREAT REGRET WE WISH TO INFORM YOU THAT ON WEDNESDAY, JULY TWENTY-THIRD, 2053, EDWIN ROBERT HALLSTROM DIED BY SUICIDE. MR. HALLSTROM IS SURVIVED BY HIS BROTHER NYLO HALLSTROM, SISTER WENDY FORTIN, NEPHEW NORTHROP HALLSTROM, AND COUSINS ARABELLA, JAYLAH, EVANDER, AND STEPHEN..."

The robotic voice went on, but I stopped listening.

All those years we spent working together, all those nights at the bar together, all those buildings we built together, all that human potential, to die alone splattered against the grill of a truck on a highway somewhere.

Maybe the Bottom Line wasn't so great after all.

That's enough phone calls for one day.

# 18

It's been two weeks since I was discharged from the hospital with a clean bill of health. Two weeks since I'd begun life as a bottom liner. Fourteen whole days of pure, unadulterated freedom. Now I can do whatever I want, just like those government ads say.

Avery and I hung out a bit during our respective recoveries. I got to know him enough to know that we probably wouldn't be very good friends. He was discharged a few days before me, and said he planned on taking it easy on the drinking for a while. I messaged him the day I was discharged, and he invited me out to the bar to celebrate my newfound health. We've messaged each other a few times, but I doubt I'll see him too often.

The warm August air brushes against my face, as much a product of nature as the wind tunnels created by the city's buildings. My legs dangle from the edge of my building's rooftop patio, a hundred and twenty three floors up. I never spent much time up here before. There's so much to see.

A transport hive floats along in the sky above. It's not much more than an old-fashioned zeppelin, a barge loaded with packages to deliver to this neighbourhood. Painted on the side of the balloon is a simple red slash against a black square. I recognize it as the emblem for DASH, an aloo delivery company.

Below the balloon is a large boat-shaped platform suspended by what I can only assume is a series of thick steel cables. The gap between the boat and the balloon leaves a space for the hundreds of delivery drones to enter and exit the hive. They must have passed by me while I was up in the crane thousands of times over the years, but I ignored them as part of the background noise.

One of them lands on a balcony below, giving me a closer look at it. It's kind of flimsy. Its two clamp-like arms hang underneath, holding a reusable plastic box large enough for a golden retriever to sit comfortably, inside which the drone carries its payload. Two larger arms rotate around it, which I assume is what's allowing it to fly. It drops the box on the balcony, picks up an identical empty one beside it, and returns to the blimp to load its box with another package for another receiver. This entire process took only a minute or so—each of these drones must deliver hundreds of packages a day.

Thinking of the logistics behind a system like this gives me a headache. I doubt a single human is involved at any point in the process.

I bet it would be fun to go for a ride on one of those zeppelins, to watch the swarm of drones from above. Maybe I could sneak onto it by hopping into one of the boxes the drone carries around. I wonder if anyone has tried that. I wonder if the drone would pick up a box and carry it, whether or not there was a human being sitting inside. Maybe it has a sensor in it to detect any movement inside the box. It's not like they have lids, so I guess it would be pretty hard to hide, though you could drape a blanket over yourself and keep really still.

However it works, there must be some sort of safety measure in place, otherwise I'm sure pets and small children would end up unintentionally abducted on a daily basis.

A collection of wind turbines whirl around me, humming and drinking up the wind. Each building has at least a few of these things seated atop it to provide cheap, renewable energy. I see them on the edges of the tops of buildings in every direction I look—my building is one of the shorter ones in the neighbourhood, how appropriate—whirling ceaselessly against the cloudless sky so vividly blue it seems painted on.

They're hypnotizing, a field of lazy soldiers quietly and tirelessly performing their assigned duty. I could watch them for hours, and have done so a lot over the past couple of weeks.

Unless I want to be a creeper and look into everyone else's windows, I either look straight up, or straight down. When I first got my condo, it had a nice view of the lake, but then they built more buildings.

I haven't projected since my return from Mars. I'm afraid to. Without an interruption, I'm worried I'll die. I could program an alarm, but considering how many times Sam's voice ended up becoming a part of my projections, I don't know if it will snap me out of it.

Maybe I'll try again in the future, once I'm stronger and I have some other distractions, someone else to snap me out of it. Maybe I could find other people who like to project and meet up with them so we could project together. That could be fun, though I've never done it with someone else before so I don't really know how that would work.

I look down at the nets installed around the edge of the building. They're made of simple mesh, forming a tilted V with the side of the building. You know what they're for, of course.

I doubt they could stop anyone who really wants to do it, though. All you have to do is leap down into the net, then climb up the side of it and hop over the edge. Or wear one of those bat suits and wait for a windy day to carry you past the net, then dive bomb the ground. Or put on a maintenance uniform and tell the people who live in the condo below the net that you need to inspect their balcony. Or skip the net altogether and just stay up here and jog in circles until the lack of oxygen makes you pass out and your brain gradually dies in the peace of sleep.

Okay, maybe the last one wouldn't work, I don't know, but the sign on the door to the balcony does suggest you don't exert yourself too much.

Not that I'm thinking of that, mind you. I don't want to give the wrong impression. I guess it's just been on my mind lately, ever since Eddie, well, you know.

I didn't go to his funeral. I would have liked to, but I didn't find out until it had already passed.

Byron told me about it a few days ago when I stopped by the job site to pick up some paperwork. Yeah, paperwork, I know. Why did I have to go all the way down there to sign a piece of paper when they could have sent everything digitally? I guess I had to go down to a government office to properly register myself so I can start getting my bottom line cheques, and even though every other place I've ever been stopped using actual paper decades ago, the government still needs you to bring paperwork and fill out forms and all sorts of nonsense at a government office.

The logic was, I heard, they'd still have all their paperwork in case of a catastrophic power failure, but if the power really did fail catastrophically, I think the world would have more important things to worry about than government records. Like, how would we connect to the internet, or how would we charge our phones, or turn the lights on, or keep our food fresh.

In many ways, the job site wasn't much different. I mean, it was different. The building is really coming along. Those aloos have done more in the last couple of weeks than the rest of us would have done in six months. But the ground, the office trailer, the shitty old food trailer, the piles of material, the tables where we used to eat lunch, it was all still there. For a moment I considered grabbing a sandwich from the food trailer, for old time's sake, before my taste buds got the better of me.

My crane was the way I had left it too, though of course I wasn't in it. Or at least I think I left it that way—I hadn't exactly been conscious, so I guess it would be more accurate to say my crane was the way I remembered it. It was in the middle of lifting a pile of steel I-beams as I walked onto the site. I had seen other cranes being operated from the ground before, but never my crane. I had a short flicker of an idea that someone had climbed up it and was messing around. Shortly after I came back to my sense, I considered climbing up there to see my old view one last time.

"HELLO, AUDEN. NICE TO SEE YOU," said a familiar robotic voice. I turned around to see one of the carpenter aloos approaching me. As it grew closer, the paint splattered across its chest became clearer until I realized it was none other than Hank. "SCANNING... FROG DETECTED. WELCOME TO THE JOB SITE."

From where I stood, I counted seven other carpenter aloos wandering around the site, though I'm sure there were more I couldn't see. One of them had something painted across its chest too, so that must have been either Clint or Blake, I couldn't tell.

"DID YOU NOT HEAR ME, AUDEN?"

Fine, okay. I'll bite.

"Hi Hank."

"DID YOU WATCH THE BLUE JAYS GAME LAST NIGHT?"

I could feel myself starting to get annoyed until I realized Hank didn't have any feelings to hurt, and I didn't need to worry about the usual social niceties. Besides, I doubt I'd ever see him again anyway.

"No, Hank, and I don't care about baseball. Get back to work, and don't ever talk to me again."

Hank turned around and walked away without a sound.

Damn, that felt good.

As I watched Hank return to the swarm of aloos crawling across the building, I heard Byron call me from his office trailer. I turned around to see his head sticking out of the window, his beard hanging down the side of the trailer like a Christmas wreath. The specks of breakfast sandwich added to the effect. I walked over to the trailer and he met me outside.

If he hadn't shouted to me, I think I'd have smelled him before I saw him. I guess it doesn't matter when your coworkers don't have any way to smell you, but I feel like it'd be unpleasant to smell yourself too.

Once he got closer, he didn't look any better. He wore his typical gruff countenance, but it had given way to something both desperate and mournful. Nostalgia too, perhaps, at seeing me—for the time when there was life on this site, and, judging by the dark circles under his eyes, for the time where he was able to sleep. Nevertheless, I'd never seen the man so animated.

I mean, compared to the average person, he was still pretty understated, but for Byron's standards he was positively jovial. I think he was trying to hide how happy he was to see me, but he wasn't doing a good job.

His demeanour shrank a little when I handed him my frog, and then a little more when he told me about Eddie's funeral. It was a small service, I guess. A few family members, some friends, and his girlfriend, held at a Catholic church, which I thought was weird since I had never known Eddie to be religious, but I guess maybe his family was. A few of the crew members were there too.

I wish I'd known about it.

Byron and I talked longer than we probably ever had that day. He told me about what the other guys were doing, which he'd already told me back at the hospital. I also learned about his dating life—I guess it's hard to date when most people your age expect you to be retired or bottom lined.

I managed not to tell him that a shower and a visit to the barbershop might make a difference.

I didn't particularly enjoy the conversation, but he seemed like he needed to be around another person, so I stuck around for awhile. Not like I had anywhere to be.

When I finally did leave, I felt like I was abandoning a dog on a desert island.

I took a look at the paperwork when I got home after I'd signed it, which was maybe not the smartest idea because who knows what I'd signed, but then again, it's not like I had a choice. If something happens to the aloo that replaced me, the company has the right to call me back to work, either temporarily or permanently. I still have to report any vacations I take to the company, so in case the crane operator aloo breaks down and they need to call me in, they know when I'm available and when I'm not. But they'd have to pay me my full rate again, so I doubt they'll bother.

I bet the only reason they got a crane aloo in the first place is because they already had the crane and they were replacing the crew wholesale. Once the crane breaks down though, I bet they won't even bother replacing it.

That's a weird thing to consider—I guess I'm like one of those guys that walked around town lighting the gas lamps along the street before they invented electric lights. I wouldn't mind being called back in, though. It might be fun. The last time I was up there, I hadn't realized I'd never do it again. It would have been nice to properly take it all in, to enjoy the cabin one last time.

You'd think you'd be able to see everything from the hundred and twenty third floor of a building, but surprisingly, one of the most interesting things is how restricted the view is. The only real direction I can see in is west. Everything else is blocked out by the other skyscrapers nearby, including the CN Tower, which everyone still thinks of as part of the iconic Toronto skyline even though the only place you can really see it anymore is if you're standing at its base or looking down from an airplane.

They should have prevented development in front of it to keep the look.

As it stands, it doesn't serve much of a purpose anymore. It doesn't work as a radio tower, considering the rest of the buildings are much taller, and who uses the radio anymore anyway?

Looking down at the ground from up here, you can barely make out anything. I mean, if you really focus, you can sometimes make out people walking on the sidewalk, but they're so tiny it's like trying to spot a fly on an apple in the fruit stand across the street. The cars you can see, but they're so predictable in their motion, like blood flowing through vessels or salmon swimming in a stream. And because most of the cars on the road now are either aloo-cabs or privately owned but self driving, you don't even get to enjoy the excitement of the occasional car crash.

I tried writing down some of my projections, too. But it turns out that's not as fun as imagining them.

Mateah called me the other day, and told me about the company she started with Kay. They're making LifeSim games. Kay's doing the art and Mateah is taking care of the coding. They're set up in Mateah's garage, actually. It reminds me of those old pictures of Silicon Valley startups from the 1990's. Just a big table down the middle of the room, with a few computers and chairs along it, plus a couple of LifeSim rigs along the wall to test their new creations.

Except this time, it's Bottom Line money bankrolling it, instead of rich parents or angel investors.

They even had an empty arcade cabinet in the corner too—Mateah said they were working on a new arcade game, and Arya said they could put it in The Black Cat when it was ready.

You played as a unicorn flying through space, which seems like at least a quarter's worth of fun, I guess. I tried one of the LifeSim rigs on and it was kind of fun too. I don't want to get one though, for the same reason I haven't done any projecting since I got out of the hospital. Maybe I could help them write their games, or come up with ideas, I don't know. But my ideas only ever seem to come alive in my head. When I try and write them down, they seem so flat. Maybe I could take a writing class or something.

I asked them why they decided to start a business. That's a reasonable question, right? They have their Bottom Line cheques coming in, after all, so they obviously don't need the money. And besides, there are already games being developed by aloos. They're not as good as the ones humans make—not yet, anyway—but they're getting there.

It's only a matter of time before they get bottom lined from that gig too. But I guess they like making games. It's hard to think about someone who runs a business because they enjoy it, but I guess it makes sense. The other guys have all found something to do I guess, and they're enjoying themselves, I guess. So why not Kay and Mateah?

But the other guys have hobbies, right? I guess building video games can be a hobby too, but when you talk about running it like a business that's a different story, I think. Or maybe it isn't, and I'm over thinking it.

Oh, and Kay reminded me they couldn't be bottom lined from their own business unless they wanted to be. Which I guess I never considered. Maybe I should start a business too, though I don't know what it would be about.

A handful of aloos clean the outside windows of the building to the north of mine.

I wonder if window washers had the same feeling dangling from the side of a building as I did up in the crane. I wonder if they feel the same way I do now. Maybe there's a group of ex–window washers I could go hang out with or something.

I'm considering calling an aloo-cab to go somewhere, but I don't have anywhere to be.

# ACKNOWLEDGEMENTS

*The Bottom Line* wasn't written in a vacuum. I owe a tremendous debt of gratitude to several key people in my life, without whom etc. In no particular order:

To my writing circle – Jenny, Naomi, Andrew – and my early readers – Tracy, Quinelle, Kate, and Allie. You helped me refine my ideas and turn my verbal vomit into something people might actually want to vread. There are entire chapters of this book which would never have been written if not for your input.

To D'arcy, thanks for explaining to me what the life of a construction worker on a high-rise is like. As a lifelong bookish nerd, that insight was invaluable.

To Justin, I know you didn't plan it this way, but Black Cat Espresso Bar was as close to the ideal place to write a book as I could imagine. Thank you for starting your business where and when you did. And thank you to the café flies I'd met there over the years I spent writing this book, and who didn't consider me rude if I come in, say hi, and hide in the corner to work. Francesco, Rocco, Richard, Laura, Steve, Miles, Sugeidy, Azu, Ellie, Naoko, George, Sep, John, Mir, and anyone I missed – each of you have left a simulacrum of yourselves on this book.

To Corey, my comrade, my brother in arms. The lifestyle we built for ourselves allowed me the time to write this thing. Our regular chats about philosophy, psychology, and life all filtered into this book in some form or another. I'm looking forward to many more collaborations in the future.

To my mom, who, after watching me lie on the ice making snow angels instead of playing hockey like I was supposed to, recognized that I was never going to be a "sports kid" and encouraged my creative side. Thank you for the unconditional love, support, and encouragement over the years.

To Lis and Vraeyda Literary, for believing in me enough to spend time and money publishing The Bottom Line. I can't possibly express my gratitude enough.

To Azima, my love, my heart, my home. Thanks for believing in me and supporting my creative pursuits.

And finally, to you, the reader. For whatever reason, you decided to spend your time with the characters in this book. I hope you enjoy their company.

If you have any questions or comments about *The Bottom Line*, I'd love to hear them. My email is sbedwards5@gmail.com.

In gratitude,

S.B. Edwards

# ABOUT SB EDWARDS

Söphie (S.B.) Edwards is a Canadian writer, historian, and voice feminization coach.

She's the host of *We Have Always Existed*, a video essay series that explores the rich history of transgender people in the ancient Mediterranean and Near East.

Söphie is a transgender woman who lives in Toronto with her girlfriend and their five cats Bean, Ella, Midna, Charlie, and Cinder.

# ALSO BY VRAEYDA

Can You Hear the Angels Sing?
Rev Prof Seth Ayettey

Aegis
RL Arenz III

NEON Lieben
Judge of Mystics Saga 1: Char & Ash
Judge of Mystics Saga 2: Son of Abel
Judge of Mystics Saga 3: Book of Revels
Sapha Burnell

Vostok
Łukasz Drobnik

My Heart is The Tempest
Sacha Rosel

Sky Tracer
Hayden Moore

Girl of Light
Elana Gomel

The Saga of Ádís Rauðfeld
Siobhán Clark

Macabre and Monstrous
Emily Armstrong, KS Bishoff, Sapha Burnell

Dustria
Madhurika Sankar

Usurper Kings
Sapha Burnell

Warning Light Calling
Peter Graarup Westergaard

The Drake Equation
Bradley Earl Hoge

Digital Desires
AJ Dalton

www.ingramcontent.com/pod-product-compliance
Ingram Content Group UK Ltd.
Pitfield, Milton Keynes, MK11 3LW, UK
UKHW042058131224
452457UK00004B/332